The Triplets and the Power of the Old School

An Old Schoolhouse Mystery
Book Two

The Triplets and the Power of the Old School—An Old Schoolhouse Mystery

Copyright © 2018 by Tim Tweedie

Credits

Cover art & illustrations © Tim Tweedie

LCN   2018906093
ISBN 978-1-945539-25-1

The Triplets and the Power of the Old School

An Old Schoolhouse Mystery
Book Two

Tim Tweedie

Dunecrest Press

This book is dedicated
to my six exceptional grandchildren
who are avid readers and the inspiration
behind the Old Schoolhouse Mysteries.
And to my wonderful wife, Judy and my
amazing brother, Jim, for doing so much to
help me put the story together for
publication.

Contents

Chapter 1   Proceed with Caution   1

Chapter 2   Field Trip to 1846   12

Chapter 3   Arnold and North   28

Chapter 4   The Lion   44

Chapter 5   The Creekside Mine   56

Chapter 6   Snatched   75

Chapter 7   Ned Steward   85

Chapter 8   Jud Day   105

Chapter 9   The Tunnel   125

Chapter 10   The Cavern   147

Chapter 11   The Party   162

Chapter 12   Powers Discovered   176

Chapter 13   The Search   197

Chapter 14   Terry   216

Chapter 15   Rebellion   231

Chapter 16   Preparation   247

Chapter 17   The Tour   261

Chapter 18   Cryptic   271

Chapter One

Proceed with Caution

The dark shapes of six people could be seen within the storage room in the back of the Hawkins's hardware store. It was late at night and the meeting was obviously meant to be secret.

"I tell you, there's not much more I can do," Pete Rider argued. "You all know I tried to buy the old school and land for a generous price, but the school board decided not to sell after the triplets had their say.

"Then I planned to rezone my thirty-acre apple orchard next to the old school and build inexpensive apartment housing. The kids from the families that moved in would be all over the old school playground. The triplets wouldn't be able to get close to the merry-go-round to take their magical field trips. I was even going to fence along the river between my property and theirs so they'd have a hard time even getting to the playground!"

"So, you try again!" a stern voice from the far side of the room interjected.

"Yeah, Pete, there's got to be another way," an older male voice bellowed in.

"Sam, I told you. The triplets have information

about me and my family that could destroy me in this community. They said they'd use it to stop me from harming the old school," Pete quickly answered back.

"Threats have never stopped you before," exclaimed Evelyn Hawkins.

"You don't understand. They can time travel," Pete added.

"We all know about the random field trips they can take through time," another male voice sputtered from the shadows.

"Those field trips are what he wants us to stop," another female voice added.

"Phil, Mabel, that's just it. Now they can control where they go on field trips! They even traveled back in time and found me at the old school when I was nine. One of them, Mikaia, even talked to me and asked me questions. I didn't know who she was until she told me a few days ago. They can even change history if they want!" Pete Rider added with a shaky voice.

Nervous gasps could be heard from around the darkened storage room.

"They've learned how to do that?" asked Phil Steward, a short stout man.

"Enough!" rang out from the far side of the room. "Cryptic will be very angry now. That threatens him and his plans to control. If they can choose where they travel in time we must find a way to stop them!" a high pitched female voice yelled out.

"They could always just disappear," Sam Hawkins said with a smile.

"Triplets suddenly missing! That wouldn't get national attention would it?" the high pitched female voice said in disgust.

"You know we can't harm them. Only Cryptic himself could possibly do that. As long as the three have pure hearts and caring souls and stick together, we can't touch them. If we can break their innocence and get them to become his Followers, then they can be destroyed, just like all of us if we don't serve him well. Since changing them seems unlikely, we have to find a way to destroy their means of time traveling without incriminating ourselves. Once the old school and playground are gone, these new custodians will be harmless. They won't be able to time travel and they'll be just like any other sixth grade children in Opportunity. I can't believe you've allowed them to gain this knowledge and power after only being here several weeks!" the high pitched female voice concluded.

"They've had help! We know that somehow they've been in contact with Halo and maybe even the Master Inventor!" Sam sang out in hopes of absolving himself from Cryptic's and their leader's wrath.

"The Master Inventor? I doubt if he would deal directly with three children. Yet you must be right about his guide, Halo. He could be teaching the three of them about the power of the old school. This is no accident!" continued the high pitched stern voice. "This must stop! Find a way to stop them from time traveling! Find a way to destroy the power of the old school!"

The triplets had just finished breakfast and were hanging out together in Mikaia's upstairs bedroom. They had been talking about the start of school in four weeks and how fast the first few weeks of summer had gone since their move from San Francisco to the old California gold rush town of Opportunity.

"Hey kids," their mother, Cathy, called up the stairs. "Your dad and I have to run into town to get a part for our air conditioner. It's going to be a hot one today, so we want to get it fixed right away. Do you want to ride in with us?"

The triplets all looked at each other for a moment without expressing much enthusiasm for the prospect. Finally, Mikaia yelled back down, "Thanks Mom, but it looks like we're going to stay."

"Yeah," Jonathan added. "If it's going to be that hot and the air conditioner isn't working, I think I'm heading for a swim in the canal or the creek."

"Okay, suit yourselves. We'll be back in a couple of hours," their mom's voice trailed off as she walked out the door.

"Hey, Jonathan, that does sound like a plan," Nicholas enthusiastically agreed. "What did you have in mind?"

"Remember that unexpected flume-ride you took the other day where the canal water runs down the hill into the creek?"

"How could I forget that? I'm still a little dizzy...but what a ride!" Nicholas returned.

"I thought I'd take a shot at it! That would sure cool me off," Jonathan answered back.

"Have you forgotten that Nicholas was lucky not to get full of slivers and a concussion when he hit the bottom, Jonathan?" mentioned Mikaia.

"Well he didn't, did he? Besides I've got all that worked out."

"Okay, what have you got in mind, Jonathan?" Mikaia asked quickly.

"That's easy. I'm wearing jean cut-offs to protect my delicate posterior from any splinters and my bike helmet to protect my head from bumping against the sides of the wooden flume," Jonathan said with a pleased smile.

"See, Mikaia, no worries," Nicholas chimed in. "He's got it all figured out. Let's get our stuff and head for the flume!"

"I still don't think this is such a great idea, but if it will cool me off, I'm all for that!" Mikaia returned as she slipped on some jean shorts and grabbed a towel when her brothers headed to their rooms to get theirs.

The siblings ran out the front door and through the trees behind their house and to the pasture. They turned north up a slight hill where the irrigation canal ran along most of the twenty acres that made up their property. Near the back of the property, just before it sloped down to a creek, the canal turned north running another couple hundred feet before the water shot down a long wooden flume splashing into the creek below.

"This is what I've been waiting for," Jonathan exclaimed as he slipped his bike helmet on and jumped into the canal a few feet before it made its descent down the flume.

"Better be cautious the first time down," Mikaia yelled out. Jonathan nodded back then proceeded to grab both sides of the flume and give himself an extra push down its wooden slide.

"See....aaaaah," was all they heard him say as he shot down the hill, almost disappearing in the spray of flying water. Then they heard something like a large rock splashing into the creek's small pond below.

It was silent as Nicholas and Mikaia peered down the hill and tried to see if Jonathan was all right. Suddenly they heard a loud "Yahoooo" coming from the pond.

"You're next Nicholas!" he yelled.

A big smile crossed his face as Nicholas bounded into the top of the flume and shoved off, throwing both arms in the air as though he were riding a giant roller coaster.

"The second time's better than the first!" Mikaia could hear him yelling as he plunged into the pond below.

"Your turn, Mikaia!" Nicholas yelled.

Mikaia fastened the clasp on her bike helmet. She slipped into the canal just before it turned down the flume, trying to slow herself down a bit as the water pushed behind her. Now as she actually sat in the flume slide, she could see that it was steeper than it had looked when she was standing outside watching. Her grip tightened against the wooden sides as she tried to decide whether it was such a good idea to let go. She started down anyway as the rushing water against her back made the decision for her. Everything was a wet blur.

Her brothers watched the screaming spray as it sped down the flume towards them and nimbly jumped aside as Mikaia pounded into the pond.

Again, there was silence as a very wet and dazed Mikaia stood up.

"Well?" asked Nicholas standing chest deep in the water next to her.

Mikaia slowly climbed out of the pond and onto the creek bank as her brothers stood there watching. She paused for a moment then started running back up the hill. Nicholas and Jonathan looked at each other as Mikaia screamed back at them, "First one up the hill gets to go again!" With that they both jumped out of the pond and tried to catch up with her.

Later the three of them sat in the shade next to the creek pond below the flume.

Jonathan kept twisting around to check his bottom for splinters, sure that he had a couple in a most uncomfortable spot.

"A great way to cool off, don't you think?" Nicholas exclaimed as a content smile graced his face.

"Not a bad idea, huh guys?" Jonathan returned wanting some credit for his suggestion as he checked the back of his jean shorts one last time.

"Our own water slide in our own back yard! Good going, Jonathan!" said Mikaia.

"You know, I wonder what Pete Rider is going to do next," Nicholas said quietly as he looked across the creek.

"What brought that on, Nicholas?" asked Jonathan.

"Well that's his property on the other side of the creek. That's where he wanted to build the apartments. I keep wondering what he and the other Followers of Cryptic will do next to stop us from taking field trips."

"That's a good question," Mikaia replied. "I can't see them trying something else to destroy the power of the old school. I don't think Pete will want to do anything after we told him what we were capable of doing to him. The other Followers like the Hawkins, I don't know."

"I say no news is good news, but we still need to

keep our eyes open. Hey, how about taking a random field trip? You know we can travel somewhere in time just to see where it takes us and what we can learn. It will be fun trying to figure out whose Essence we'd be following," Jonathan said excitedly.

"The power of the old school," repeated Nicholas.

"What's that for?" Jonathan said as he looked over.

"You ever wonder where the power to time travel comes from when we use the swing, slide, or merry-go-round to take our field trips?"

"Yeah, it was all worked out by William Lowe when he built the school in 1860, with a little help from the Master Inventor," Jonathan said with a smile.

"I see your point, Nicholas. It can't just be magic. The power has to come from somewhere," Mikaia said also deep in thought.

"It's got to come from somewhere in or near the old school for it to let the playground equipment send us off," Nicholas returned.

"Well, if Cryptic's Followers haven't been able to figure it out and destroy it after all these years, the chance of us finding how it works is pretty slim," replied Jonathan.

"Yeah, but it's still worth looking..." Nicholas paused and looked up the hill across the creek from them.

"I've got this strange feeling that someone is

watching us," he continued.

Jonathan and Mikaia also looked up into the trees on the hillside above them.

"Now that you mention it, I thought I saw something move up there just before I started down the flume, but I figured it was just my adrenaline kicking in," Mikaia said as she continued to search the trees.

"Maybe you're both still dizzy from the rides down," suggested Jonathan.

"Could be, but I still have this feeling," Nicholas returned.

"Who cares if somebody is watching us. They probably wish they were cooling off down here with us. Besides let's get back to that field trip I want to take. Is it a go?" Jonathan asked.

"I'm game," Mikaia chimed in as she stood up. "But first I want to change out of these wet clothes."

"Count me in. It sounds like another exciting adventure. I wonder where we'll end up this time?" replied Nicholas as he slowly started back up the hill towards home.

When they got back to the house to change, their mom and dad hadn't returned yet. Mikaia left a note for them explaining that after their swim they had decided to head over to the old school to play.

"That note's a good idea, Mikaia," Nicholas reasoned. "Not only will they know where we're going to be, it will also keep them from coming to look for us when we might be in the middle of a field trip."

"Good point," added Jonathan. "Now let's move out."

"Did you bring the school roster of the kids who attended the old school between 1860 and 1930?" Nicholas asked Mikaia.

"Yep, got it right here in my pocket, so let's go!"

Chapter Two

Field Trip to 1846

As they crossed the creek and hiked up through the trees that bordered the old apple orchard, no one said a word. They all kept looking around to see if someone had been watching them. When they got to the top, they tried to look through the over-grown orchard towards the old school, but all they could see was the school house bell tower above the trees about a hundred yards away.

"I don't see anyone," Jonathan was first to say.

"Let's move through the orchard slowly until we can get a good look at the school and playground," Mikaia suggested.

As they came closer, Jonathan spoke up again. "I still don't see anyone. I think it's about time we jumped on the merry-go-round."

"Why not the swings or slide?" asked Nicholas.

"Well the swings can only send us forward in time and the slide can only send us back, while the merry-go-round..."

"I got it," Nicholas interrupted. "The merry-go-round can send us forward or back in time, following some school kid's Essence who once touched or played on it. We have the chance to go any direction!"

"Then we've agreed to travel from the merry-go-round?" Mikaia cut in. "That's perfectly fine with me," she continued as they began to run towards it.

They all grabbed a side bar on the merry-go-round and started running around it, pushing as hard as they could. As it got going faster Mikaia, as usual, jumped on. After a couple more times around gaining speed, Jonathan jumped on. Nicholas kept running until he couldn't go any faster. Mikaia held Jonathan's hand as he reached out to pull Nicholas on. With a grab and a tug Nicholas was on as Mikaia yelled, "Hold hands and think of Midst!" With that she let go of the bar and they all spun off into the air.

Everything was a blur until they could make out the fuzzy white cotton candy swirl around them. Then everything seemed white as they softly landed on one of the clouds in Midst.

"Well, welcome back to Midst!" The triplets looked to their left and saw two small round men dressed all in white approaching. Their deep blue eyes and hair stood out against the whiteness of their clothes and the clouds.

"Hither, Yon, it's good to see you again," Mikaia said smiling at them as they approached.

"And how may I be of service to you three?" Yon asked with a big smile and slight bow.

"What do you mean, 'How can I be of service',

Yon?" interrupted Hither. "You sound like a travel agent. You know that we send them off on their field trips each time they come to Midst following someone's Essence."

"Of course I do, but it doesn't hurt to be polite and professional. We do provide a service you know and this time it's my turn since they're traveling further back in time," Yon returned.

"So, we're going further back in time on this field trip?" Nicholas quickly asked.

"I don't think you're supposed to tell them what happens next, Yon," scolded Hither.

"Didn't we already have this conversation, Hither? Didn't we decide that they already know that you, Hither, send them on field trips that are closer in time and I, Yon, send them further in time? Now they can even decide where they want to go by following the Essence of a student who once attended the old school. They just bring a personal possession of that person with them. So what difference does it make what I say? As long as I do my job and am professional about it, the Master Inventor will be pleased," Yon concluded.

"Now that you mention it, I guess we did talk a little about all that," Hither admitted.

"Then, let me do my job," returned Yon. "Now, how may I be of service to you three?"

"We're ready to get on with the field trip if you are, Yon," Jonathan interjected.

"Yes, Yon, and we do appreciate your professionalism," Mikaia added.

"See Hither? It always helps to act professionally. The clients are much more likely to be polite in return," Yon said as he looked over at Hither.

Hither just shook his head as he walked off mumbling something about being stuck in Midst with Yon.

"Very good, now are you ready?" Yon asked as the triplets all nodded yes. "Then hold hands, close your eyes...and..."

The triplets felt a strong wind blowing across them and again heard sounds like electricity sparking and hissing. Everything was white. Then it quickly turned brown and dusty as they heard someone loudly yelling, "Gee...Haw"... followed by a sharp cracking noise.

"What in the world is this?" Jonathan exclaimed as they all swung their hands back and forth trying to stop the dust from getting into their eyes.

"Everything is blurry and I can hardly see!" said Nicholas.

"Quick! Move back!" Mikaia shouted as a large covered wagon pulled by six muscular oxen nearly ran them over.

"Gee...Haw" the man walking next to the wagon yelled as he held the reins and cracked a long-lashed oxen whip over the oxen's heads. "You children better watch out where you're a-walkin' or you'll be

15

flattened in no time 'round here. It's gettin' late in the season and people are awantin' to hit the trail," he screamed above all the racket around them.

"What in the world is this? All I can see are covered wagons!

"Where are you heading?" asked Jonathan.

"Can't you read none, boy? What does the wagon say?" the man yelled back as he continued past.

The triplets could see a crude sign tacked to the canvas that covered the wagon. It said "California or Bust". A rugged looking lady in a bonnet sat on the front seat wearing a long green and brown dress. As the wagon passed, two sets of children's eyes peeked out from between the canvas slits.

"Hey!" Nicholas said excitedly. We're somewhere near the start of the Oregon-California Trail. It must be sometime in the mid 1800's. I remember reading about the wagon trains that traveled west for land and a better life."

"Yeah, I guess so. But where exactly are we? And what year is this?" Mikaia asked.

"Let's move toward that building over there and get out of the way before we get hit," suggested Jonathan.

As they moved closer they could read the sign that hung above the building.

"Independence, Missouri, Trail Supply Emporium. Wow! This is the main gathering town where the pioneers got supplies and formed wagon trains," Nicholas added.

"All I can see are covered wagons, oxen, horses, mules, and even some hand carts and buggies loaded with supplies," observed Jonathan as his eyes surveyed the chaos. "There must be at least a hundred wagons."

"I wonder whose Essence we followed," said Mikaia.

"I don't know, but it looks like a dusty and smelly mess to me," Jonathan replied.

"Careful where you're stepping," he added as he jumped between some darker brown piles on the ground.

Just then a horse ridden by a young girl almost knocked them down as she tried to dodge a small handcart that cut her off.

"Hey, be careful!" yelled Jonathan.

"Whoa," she yelled, quickly pulling up on her mount. "Sorry! I didn't mean to almost run you over. It's crazy around here. I can't wait till we get out on the trail and away from all this mess where we'll have room to breathe and ride."

"Where are you going?" Nicholas asked.

"My family and friends are heading to California. My step-father, James Reed, was a furniture maker back near Springfield, Illinois. He wants to start new in California and get my mother, who's ailing, into that nice warm climate. I'm Virginia Reed."

"Nice to meet you," said Mikaia.

"Where are you three headed? Maybe we'll all be on the same wagon train!" Virginia said with a smile.

"Oh, our family is still looking at all the choices. We're not quite sure yet," Mikaia spoke up quickly."

Just then two other girls who also appeared to be

around eleven to thirteen came running up.

"Hi Virginia, what are you doing?" the younger of the two asked.

"Just visiting. Oh, this is Leanna Donner and this is her sister Elitha."

"I'm Mikaia and these are my brothers, Nicholas and Jonathan."

"Nice to meet you," Leanna said.

Mikaia could see that Elitha was holding a small doll that looked much like her doll Friendly.

"I like your doll," Mikaia said.

"Oh, yes. It belongs to Virginia's sister, Patty," Elitha replied. "She let me hold it for a while. She's younger and she says it keeps her company on the trip."

"Do you know what the date is today?" Jonathan asked as Nicholas and Mikaia quickly looked at him.

"Well, we have to find out, don't we?" he said as he looked back.

"I lose track of time out here too. It's May 20th," Virginia said as she smiled down from her horse at Jonathan.

"What year is it?" he asked.

"You sure have lost track of time. It's 1846, of course."

The triplets looked at each other for a moment. Then Nicholas's eyes lit up like he'd just been struck by lightning.

"Is your father George Donner?" he asked as he

looked at Leanna and Elitha.

"Yes, how'd you know that?" Leanna asked.

Nicholas fumbled for a moment then spoke. "We heard his name around here and that he and some friends were looking for a good wagon train to go with to California."

"Oh, yes, the Reeds and us. Those are our three wagons over there," Leanna said as she pointed to a large group over at the side. "We have twelve yoke of oxen, five saddle horses, and some milk and beef cattle we're taking with us. My father says you can't afford to be under prepared for a trip like this. My Uncle Jacob has three wagons too."

"And those three wagons just past Leanna's are our wagons. Look, there's my dad riding his horse, Glaucus," Virginia stated as she pointed through the crowd.

"That's a beautiful horse," Jonathan said.

"Yes, my father is very fond of him," Virginia replied with a smile.

"And what is that?" Jonathan returned as his eyes caught a gigantic covered wagon moving between two smaller ones."

"The big one?" Virginia said as she turned to look. "Oh, that's a Pioneer Palace Car. My dad had it built. He wanted to make sure my mom was comfortable and we could all be together."

"It must be two stories high!" exclaimed Mikaia.

"It is, but it sure rides well," Virginia smiled.

"We've got to meet with our parents now, but after we do, we could meet you by the side of the supply store."

"Yes, we'd like that," Nicholas replied.

As the two Donner girls started running back and Virginia brought her horse to a gallop, the triplets moved closer to the store.

"I can't believe it!" Nicholas exclaimed.

"Can't believe what?" Jonathan asked.

"Don't you remember your early California history and the infamous Donner Party that got stranded by the early snows in the Sierras and half of them died?" Nicholas explained.

"Now that you mention it, yes, I do," Mikaia said.

"Yeah, isn't there a lake called Donner Lake on the way to Reno?" asked Jonathan.

"There sure is, and that's where a lot of the party got stuck and died!" Nicholas replied.

"Look at this! On the second page of the old school roster," Mikaia said as she pulled out the list. "Rebecca Donner App was a student from 1861 to 1863. It must be her Essence we're following, or the Essence of her mother, either Leanna or Elitha, who as parents probably helped at the school."

"Wow, this is scary. I don't know what we should say or tell them," Nicholas exclaimed. "If we just come out and tell them that they are doomed if they go, they'll think we're crazy and ignore what we say. We have to be careful, but we have to say something."

"Nicholas, do you remember enough about the

trip to discourage them or warn them about it without sounding like a lunatic?" asked Mikaia.

"I think so. I read a book or two about the early immigrants and the Donner Party since it interested me so much. Just about everything bad that could happen to immigrants on the Oregon-California Trail happened to them. They even left the main trail to follow a shorter route recommended by a supposed expert that cost them three weeks of time and got them snowed in among the Sierras. Historians even think they cannibalized, you know, ate those who had died, in order to survive. It's quite a tragic story of sad and heroic things. Only about half of them made it to the Central Valley of California," Nicholas explained.

"Look, here they come now. It looks like one of their mothers is coming with them. This could make it even more difficult," Mikaia said.

"Hi again," Mikaia said as she greeted them.

"This is our Mom, Tamsen Donner," Leanne said, "and these are Mikaia, Nicholas, and Jonathan, the children we just told you about."

"Nice to meet all of you. I understand your parents haven't decided yet on how they're going to get to California?"

"No ma'am," Mikaia said with a smile.

"How are you planning on traveling there?" Nicholas asked.

"Well, we are trying to join or form a wagon train, and then follow the Oregon-California Trail all the way to California," Tamsen returned with a smile. "When we get there, my husband, George, hopes to farm and I hope to open a school for girls."

"Why just girls?" Mikaia asked.

"They are of special interest to me since they usually have to go to work earlier than boys and often are not allowed to go to school past the sixth grade."

"Oh, that's the school year we are going into," Mikaia added.

"Then you're all the same age?" Tamsen asked.

"Yes, we're triplets, although not identical as you can tell," replied Mikaia.

"I like that!" Virginia who had walked back over with them replied.

"Do you have a trail map to follow?" Nicholas cut in.

"Yes, Nicholas, we do," Tamsen replied, "and an excellent guide book called *The Emigrant's Guide to Oregon and California* by a man named Lansford Hastings."

Jonathan and Mikaia could see Nicholas's eyes get big as he swallowed hard.

"I've heard of him. I've also heard that many believe that he doesn't really know what he's talking about, and that he's only traveled over the trail once," Nicholas carefully said.

"Most people think he's quite the expert," Tamsen replied.

"When we finally get going my dad says we're

going to stay on the main trail and not be persuaded or tricked into taking any supposed short-cuts. That's what he's recommending to every one after doing a lot of studying on it," Nicholas continued.

"Your dad sounds like a smart and educated man," Tamsen returned. "He is probably right. It is always best to stay with what you know until you are positive another choice is better."

"My dad says that's particularly important when you get to Sandy Point, Wyoming. He says just before the main trail splits off to the right and a smaller trail turns to the left and travels down to Fort Bridger, that we must be sure to turn right!" Nicholas exclaimed strongly.

"You certainly remember a lot about the trail that your dad has taught you. You are probably a very good student," Tamsen replied.

"Oh, he is a good student," Mikaia chimed in, "and very seldom wrong."

"We have to get back to the wagons. George has found a group that wants to head out tomorrow. I hope we will see you along the way," Tamsen said as she started back towards the wagons.

The three girls stood there for a moment, and then Virginia spoke. "It was nice to meet you. I hope we see you in California."

"Please make sure your dad takes the main trail to California. I've heard some bad things about a shortcut," Nicholas added one last time.

"We will. That way I can be with more of my friends along the way," Virginia said smiling as she walked away with Leanna and Elitha waving good-by.

"You sure tried hard to convince them to stay on the main trail, Nicholas," Jonathan said as he watched them leaving.

"I just hope it was strong enough to change their history," Nicholas replied.

"I wonder which of the two Donner girls will become the mother of Rebecca?" Mikaia asked. "At least we know that they make it to California."

"All three of the girls do. Unfortunately, Tamsen was never able to start her girls' school," Nicholas said as the others understood what he really meant.

"I'm ready to get away from all this noise and dust," Nicholas expressed suddenly.

"Yeah, it has been quite a trip. I'm ready too," Jonathan added.

"Then let's go around to the back of the building and get out of here," Mikaia said.

When the triplets got behind the trail supply building, they all held hands. Mikaia reminded them to think back to exactly where they were and what they each were thinking as they started to spin off the merry-go-round. Everything became blurry again while the fluffy cotton candy clouds swirled around them. Suddenly they sat in their desks in the old school. They were almost home.

"Welcome back!" Tique said. "I'll let you catch

your breath before we 'critique' what you have learned from your field trip."

"Thanks, Tique. That was a bit exhausting," Nicholas said as he put his head down on his desk.

"So now, what did you three learn?" Tique asked in her usual way after a few moments.

Jonathan, as always, spoke up first. "I learned that the early west was dirty and rugged and you had to be strong and lucky to survive."

"Very true, Jonathan. Things were hard back then. How about you, Mikaia?"

"I learned that people no matter where they are in history, are very much the same. They want a good life for their families and have to make hard decisions all the time. Some choices will help them prosper, but poor choices can be disastrous."

"Great insight for someone your age, Mikaia," replied Tique.

"And now you, Nicholas, what did you learn?"

"I learned that I worry a lot about other people, and that I want to try to help them whenever I can. I get frustrated when I can't help them make the right decisions...decisions that may even save their lives. I just hope that the Donner girls and their mother listened to what I had to say."

"You are very sensitive to others and a very caring soul. I understand your special concern for the people you just met. I too hope your conversations helped," Tique replied. "As always you have all learned valuable lessons which I hope you remember and share with others."

"Before you are dismissed I have a word of caution for you. I just noticed two boys outside the school hiding in the trees by the road. I'm not sure why they are here, but if they're hiding, they are probably up to no good."

"Thanks, Tique, for warning us," Mikaia said.

"What do you think we should do?" asked Nicholas.

"That's up to the three of you," Tique replied.

"I think we should climb out the back window just in case they are watching for us. We don't want them to know we were in here, especially if they didn't see us go in."

"You're right, Jonathan. Let's climb out the back and sneak around into the apple orchard. Then we'll walk back to the playground like we just got here. Maybe we can draw them out and find out what they are up too," Mikaia suggested.

Jonathan had already started for the window with Nicholas and Mikaia just behind him.

Mikaia quietly turned and said, "See you later, Tique."

As Tique smiled back she said, "By the way, class dismissed."

Chapter Three

Arnold and North

The triplets managed to get to the orchard without being spotted and started walking towards the playground.

As they did, two boys about the triplets' age jumped out from the trees just south of the merry-go-round and started walking toward them.

"Hey, did you come to play in the playground?" the taller one asked.

"Yes, we did," Jonathan said as he stepped forward. "I'm Jonathan, and these are my brother and sister, Nicholas and Mikaia. We just moved into Opportunity from San Francisco."

"Yeah, I've heard about the three of you. You're the ones who fixed up the old school and playground so that now we can even play here. I'm Arnold Hawkins and this is my friend, North."

"North? That's an unusual first name," Mikaia replied.

"Oh, yeah. We call him that because he keeps forgetting what direction he's going. So, we figured if we could get him to learn which way was north he wouldn't get lost so often. So, to remind him, we call him North," Arnold said with a slight smile as North just stood there expressionless.

"Did it help?" Jonathan asked.

"Some, but he usually just follows someone."

"So, you came to use the playground equipment too?" Nicholas asked.

"Yeah, we came to camp and play," said Arnold.

"Camp?" Nicholas replied.

"Yeah, we just put our tent and stuff over in the trees. We're going to be here until school starts. My granddad, Sam Hawkins, is paying us to hang around here and let him know what we see. He brings us water and great meals two times a day!" Arnold said with a wink.

The triplets looked at each other for a moment realizing that this must be the next thing Cryptic's Followers were doing to stop their field trips.

"We would have spent some nights here too if it wasn't for the mountain lion," Jonathan quickly replied.

"The mountain lion?" North, finally coming to life, asked.

"Yeah," Jonathan responded. "We'd heard that one was in the area most nights looking for food and that it even ate a large goat at a ranch up the hill a-ways. So, we decided we'd just come here during the day."

North swallowed hard obviously not liking the idea of spending nights at the old school with a lion on the prowl.

"The poor lion's probably more afraid of us than we are of him. Besides we can always scare him off if he comes near," Arnold returned.

"Really, I just hope none of that food your grandmother is cooking for you has any gravy or something that smells good that might attract that lion," Jonathan added.

"You don't worry about us. We can take care of ourselves," Arnold said as he threw out his chest.

"What kind of food is your grandfather bringing us tonight anyway?" North asked, quite uncomfortable with the situation.

"I don't know, but it's nothing to worry about," replied Arnold, quite annoyed that his buddy was sounding so concerned.

"Didn't you three come to play?" Arnold added changing the conversation away from the lion.

"We sure did," Nicholas quickly responded. "See you around."

The triplets ran over to the swings and slide.

"What lion are you talking about, Jonathan? I know there are some around but I haven't heard of anyone seeing one for a long time," Mikaia asked.

"Me neither," Jonathan replied, "but they don't need to know that."

"Good going, Jonathan. "That should keep them

thinking tonight. Maybe we can scare them away, otherwise it will be hard to take field trips for a while," Nicholas said as he jumped onto a swing and started pumping.

Mikaia sat in the swing next to him while Jonathan slid a couple of times down the slide before joining them in the third swing.

"I still can't figure out where the power to time travel comes from. It's got to be around here somewhere," Nicholas said. "I want to spend some time searching in and around the old school."

"How do you expect to do that when we're so closely watched?" asked Mikaia looking towards the trees. Arnold and North were sitting in the shade near the small tent they had just erected.

"We could slip back into the school through the back window that we just climbed out of," Nicholas returned.

"I'm game!" replied Jonathan.

"I think we should sneak back later when they don't think we're around. They just might come looking when they don't see us playing anymore," advised Mikaia.

"You're right. Besides a trip into town may answer some questions for us," Nicholas suggested.

"Like what?" Jonathan asked.

"If we could talk to Bill Peters we might find out what he knows about the old school and where the power to travel comes from. He is keeping an eye on

Cryptic's Followers for us. We could try to get to Midst and call Halo. I'm sure he knows a lot about it. But since that's not an option right now, let's see Mr. Peters."

"Good idea," Jonathan replied, "and I think a trip back to the antique store is in order."

"What do you have in mind, Jonathan?" asked Mikaia.

"I don't really know, but I'll know it when I see it!"

The triplets headed towards the orchard with Mikaia waving goodbye to the two boys. North started to wave back, but Arnold quickly grabbed his hand.

"I guess we did see something moving on the hill across the creek earlier," Mikaia said.

"Probably Arnold and North watching us," Jonathan replied.

"They are quite a pair!" Mikaia stated as she shook her head.

"Yeah, but they've sure created a big problem for us," Nicholas said as they headed down toward the creek.

When they approached the house, the triplets could see the Odyssey parked in front. Their dad, with a big frown on this face, was coming out of the front door.

"What's the matter, Dad?" Mikaia asked.

"Just my luck, our air conditioner is a special heavy-duty unit that Harold Lowe must have bought from the same company that makes them for the schools, so I need to go back to the hardware store and get another part. Darn, a simple project becomes a bigger one."

"Could we ride in with you?" Nicholas asked.

"Sure, but I have to come back right away."

"That's all right. We'll just walk home. It's only about two miles," Nicholas replied.

"Well suit yourselves. Just tell your mom you're coming with me and hop on in."

Jonathan immediately ran into the house returning about three minutes later.

"Mom says it's fine with her, but that we shouldn't stay in town too long," Jonathan reported.

Their dad parked on the street in front of the hardware store and went inside as the triplets walked down the street to the Bank of Opportunity.

When they peeked in the front window they could see Mr. Peters working at his desk.

"Good morning! How may I help you?" the young lady receptionist asked.

"We'd like to speak to Mr. Peters for a moment," Mikaia answered.

"Unless you've scheduled an appointment I'm afraid Mr. Peters is..."

"Hey, the Frazier triplets! Come on in," a loud voice from the back-office declared.

"I guess Mr. Peters is available," the receptionist said with a smile as she walked them back to Mr.

Peter's office.

"Have a seat. What can I do for you?" Mr. Peters asked quickly closing his door.

"Well first of all we just met Arnold Hawkins. He and a friend are being paid by Arnold's grandfather to camp out at the old school and report back to him anything they see," Mikaia replied. "So, our field trips seem to be on hold for a while."

Mr. Peters leaned back in his chair shaking his head a bit.

"So that's their next step to slow you three down," he said as a smile began to appear. "You really have them buffaloed. They're not quite sure how to counteract you. That's a good sign, but I'm sure they're looking for other ways to stop you and destroy your power to time travel."

"We can take care of Arnold and his friend, North, Mr. Peters," Jonathan said as the other two stared at him in surprise.

"What we really need to know is how time travel is powered? It can't just jump out of the playground equipment. We thought you might know something about it. We can't protect it if we don't know what to protect," Nicholas continued.

"You're right there. The problem is that even though I took field trips, I was never able to discover its power. Fortunately, neither have Cryptic or his Followers. If they knew, it would have been destroyed long ago."

"Hasn't Halo said anything to you about it?" Mikaia asked. "We'd ask him ourselves but we can't travel to Midst without Arnold seeing us."

"We have had some conversations about it. We speculate that William Lowe, with information from the Master Inventor, somehow built the power into or close by the old school in 1859. I've poked around off and on for years but haven't found the answer. A lot of building and mining activity was going on all around Opportunity in those days so few people would have paid much attention when the old school was built."

"We appreciate your help, Mr. Peters. I guess we'll just have to look around a bit too," Mikaia said as she stood up.

"You all do need to be careful. I know that Sam and Evelyn Hawkins along with Pete Rider and Phil and Mabel Steward are Followers. We've been keeping an eye on them. But there is someone else in town who is a Follower and maybe even their leader whom I haven't discovered yet."

"What do you mean, 'we've been keeping an eye'?" Jonathan asked.

"There are other people in town who are friends of the Master Inventor. They are helping me, but they prefer to remain nameless at this time," Mr. Peters replied.

"Just who are Phil and Mabel Steward?" asked Nicholas.

"Oh, yes. You may remember them from the school board meeting at which the three of you spoke up. They were the couple who supported Pete's bid to buy the old school and tear it down. Phil's a retired mining engineer from the Mariposa area, who like his father and grandfather, was born and raised here, moved to Mariposa, and then returned with his wife about ten years ago. They keep a low profile but I know they would do almost anything they were directed to do by Cryptic or their leader here in Opportunity."

"I do remember them, " Nicholas replied. "Thanks for warning us, Mr. Peters. We'll try and keep an eye out for them too."

"More Followers," Jonathan said as they stepped outside. "I hope that's all of them."

"Me too," added Mikaia. "The worst thing is that we still have no idea where the power to time travel comes from."

"I say let's go to the antique store," Jonathan suggested.

"Fine with me. There is a lot of interesting stuff in there. Maybe they even have some more old bottles I could buy for my collection," Nicholas added with a smile.

"You and your bottles," Mikaia said as she turned and headed towards the antique shop.

When they entered the shop, Terry walked over to them.

"Good to see you three again," she said with a nice smile. "Did you come for more bottles and historical documents or a doll for Mikaia's collection?"

"Actually, just to look around a bit," Jonathan said

"Well, you're welcome to stay as long as you like."

Mikaia walked to the back to check out the old dolls as Nicholas headed towards the old bottle section. Jonathan moved over to a rack full of music CDs and put on a headphone to listen to the one that was playing. He smiled as the sounds of wind, thunder and falling water were played on the "Sounds of the Sierras" CD. All of a sudden, his eyes lit up as he picked up the CD "Animals of the Sierras." He quickly put the new disc on and listened. After a few minutes he put the disc back in its case and walked over to Mikaia.

"Mikaia, do you still have the old battery-operated boom box that plays CDs?"

Mikaia looked at him for a moment with a questioning expression. Knowing Jonathan, he could have a hundred reasons for the question so she just answered "Yes, it's in my closet."

"Thanks," replied Jonathan looking back at her with a big grin.

He walked over the section that held old newspapers, magazines, and other documents where Nicholas was going through a stack of papers.

"Find anything interesting?" Jonathan asked.

"There's all kinds of neat stuff here. I can see why you started an historical document collection. I'm thumbing through a stack of old mining claims. Some go as far back as the early 1850's! Look at this one, 'The Timber Pine Mining Claim filed by D.C. Powers'. It looks like it even describes the location and how much land the claim covers," Nicholas said as he knelt down and picked up a pile of old land deeds.

"I might buy a couple of those for my documents collection," Jonathan stated as he also started looking through the stack. He picked out one from 1858 and another claim from 1852 before taking them over to Terry.

"How much are this CD and these two mining claims?" he asked

"The CD is eleven dollars and each mining claim is five."

"So, a total of twenty-one dollars plus tax?" he returned.

"Yes, that should do it," Terry replied as Jonathan pulled a twenty and a ten-dollar bill from his pocket mumbling that he hoped it was worth the money.

As they walked outside Jonathan said, "Well, I still have my change from the thirty dollars I gave to Terry."

Mikaia looked at him and said "So?"

"So, the last one to the ice cream and candy store is last in line," he yelled as he darted down the sidewalk with Nicholas and Mikaia close behind.

They stood in line behind Jonathan as he ordered his usual double chocolate chip cone. Mikaia looked at Nicholas and put her empty hands up as Nicholas quickly put his into his pockets looking for money.

"When did you have time to pick up some money?" Mikaia asked Jonathan who was licking on his cone.

"I grabbed some when I ran back in the house to tell Mom we were going with Dad."

"Well thanks. We don't have any with us," Mikaia said with a frown.

Jonathan stopped licking for a moment and looked at them and then back at his cone.

"I guess I could lend you some money. I still have six dollars in change."

Nicholas and Mikaia were now both frowning at Jonathan.

"Okay, okay! It's on me this time, but I'm keeping track," he muttered as Mikaia ordered a single scoop of rocky road and Nicholas ordered his favorite, mint chip.

Just then two girls came into the store and walked up to the counter. When they saw the triplets, one whispered something to the other then they both smiled. Mikaia, who was closest to them, spoke up.

"Hi, I'm Mikaia and these are my brothers, Nicholas and Jonathan."

Both boys smiled and nodded as they continued working on their cones.

Finishing off their cones, they started
walking back home.

"Yes, we've heard of the Frazier triplets already. I'm Ashlee Wilson and this is Marie Jimenez. We'll all be at Lowe Middle School together in a few weeks. We may even be in the same classes since we're going into the sixth grade too."

"That will be great! We've been looking forward to meeting kids who'll be going to school with us," replied Mikaia.

"How long have you been living in Opportunity?" Nicholas asked between licks.

"I was born here and Marie's family came here from Mexico ten years ago," Ashlee replied.

"Yes, my family picked grapes in the valley until they had enough money to buy a small vineyard just outside of town. I really like it here," Marie said.

"It was nice meeting both of you," Mikaia replied.

"If you want us to show you all the middle school hangout spots sometime, let us know," Ashlee offered. "My name's in the phonebook."

"Thanks, we'll do that," Mikaia replied as she and her brothers left the shop.

"They seemed nice," Nicholas said.

"Yeah, they were even cute," replied Jonathan as Mikaia and Nicholas looked over at him and smiled.

Finishing off their cones, they started walking back along the road towards home.

"Jonathan, why did you buy that CD?" Nicholas asked.

"I call it 'the problem solver'," he returned.

"All right, Jonathan," Mikaia said. "I can't wait to hear this. What problem are you going to solve?"

"Arnold and North, of course."

"How in the world are you..." Mikaia started to say.

"'Animal Sounds of the Sierras,'" that's how," Jonathan quickly replied.

"What did you find, Jonathan? Sounds of owls and blue jays?" Mikaia asked.

"No! Something much better...Mountain lion roars and purrs, something which I plan on playing tonight at the old school after I borrow your boom box!"

"Great idea, Jonathan!" Nicholas replied.

"You had me going on that one, Jonathan," Mikaia said with a smile. "I'm game."

"I figured we'd sneak out about midnight and play a few mountain lion songs for the boys," Jonathan said as he swallowed the last of his cone. "They should be asleep by then and I'm sure they'd love to be awakened by the sounds of nature. If this works, we could take a field trip tomorrow."

"Then we could go to Midst and see what Halo knows about the power of the old school," Mikaia added.

"Before we do that I think we should look in the four trunks Harold Lowe, or as we know now, Halo, left in our attic when he moved," Nicholas suggested.

"We've been through those trunks several times. What would we be looking for?" asked Mikaia.

"Another clue. So far we've found things like Pete Rider's third grade cap and Harold Lowe's head custodian name plate that have led us right to them. It's almost like Halo planted things in the trunk for us to find which have helped us gather information and increase our power to time travel," Nicholas explained.

"You're right, Nicholas. Another look could turn up something else," Jonathan replied.

"I'm especially interested in that fourth trunk, the one filled with school supplies and old books," stated Nicholas.

Just then they saw a fast-moving pickup truck zoom by, heading up the road leading to the old school.

"That looked like Sam Hawkins to me," Mikaia said.

"That was him," added Jonathan.

"Looks like an early dinner is on its way to Arnold and North," Nicholas replied.

"I hope they enjoy their evening, at least until we get there," Jonathan said as they all laughed heartily.

Chapter Four

The Lion

When Nicholas, Jonathan, and Mikaia arrived home, they immediately headed towards the attic. As they passed by the kitchen, their mom told them that dinner would be ready in thirty minutes.

They climbed the stairs, pushed open the attic door and went in. Nicholas plugged in the extension cord that led to the light they had placed just above the trunks which sat near the back wall. A little light still streamed in through the small attic window.

"Okay, now what exactly are we looking for?" Jonathan asked.

"It's kind of like you and your historical documents, Jonathan. You just don't know until you see it and you can put the clues together," Nicholas replied. "Why don't you and Mikaia look through the first three trunks and I'll go through the one with the school supplies."

"Fine with me," replied Mikaia as she opened the second trunk, since Jonathan was already tossing around stuff from the first.

Nicholas pulled out a stack of *Dick and Jane* reading books and also a couple of books for teachers on how to teach basic math and science. After he removed a pile of student chalk boards, he was able to get a better view of the other things that lined the bottom of the trunk. Old pens, along with the sealed ink bottles in which to dip them, and some boxes of chalk lay flat along the bottom next to several piles of lined paper.

"Hey, this looks like fun!" he said as he picked up a small brass school hand bell and began to ring it. "That's strange. The sound makes my whole body vibrate!"

"It sounds like the dinner bell to me!" Jonathan exclaimed. "I'm sure Mom's ready for us by now."

"Always thinking with your stomach, Jonathan," Mikaia said as she continued to look through her trunk.

"A man has to eat you know. That old bell does have a nice sound to it," Jonathan admitted kneeling down next to the third trunk.

A lot of other school supplies and materials were in the fourth trunk but nothing that seemed to catch Nicholas's interest. As he started putting things back in the trunk, he noticed a paper between the pages of the basic science teacher's manual. He opened the book to that page and took the folded paper out. Immediately his eyes lit up.

"Now we're talking," he said as he looked over the

paper.

"What did you find?" asked Mikaia as she scooted over next to him.

"Hey, Jonathan, what does this look like to you?" Nicholas asked.

Jonathan was right behind him trying to catch enough light on the paper so he could read it. "That's an old mining claim like the ones I bought from Terry!"

"Yeah, but do you see whose names are on it?" Nicholas returned.

Jonathan squinted in the dim light then said loudly, "W. Lowe and D. C. Powers!"

"Together they staked a claim on the Creekside Mine!" replied Nicholas.

"That's got to be William Lowe! Look at the date, 1858," Mikaia added.

"Jonathan, isn't D.C. Powers the name we saw on one of the other old claims in the antique store today?" Nicholas asked.

"I remember, yeah, something like the Timber something Mining Claim."

"Then William Lowe and D.C. Powers must have done some mining business together. Maybe Mr. Powers helped William Lowe build the old school in 1860," Nicholas added.

By now Mikaia had picked up the science book that lay open on the floor and was busy reading.

"What do you think this all means, Mikaia?"

Jonathan asked.

"I think it's another clue left by Harold Lowe...along with this book," she added.

"What's so important about the book?" asked Jonathan.

"The paper marked the start of a chapter on magnets and magnetic attraction. Further on it talks about magnets and light."

"So?" Jonathan returned.

"I don't know, but these trunks seem to be full of clues. I think we should read this chapter at least and see where it leads."

"And I think we should head back to town and buy the mining claim document of D.C. Powers. There could be a connection between this claim and that one," Jonathan suggested.

"I think you're right. Even if there isn't, at least you'll have another old claim for your collection," Nicholas added.

Suddenly Jonathan said, "I'm going downstairs."

"What's the hurry?" Nicholas asked.

"Dinner!" Jonathan replied as he moved towards the door.

"How do you know?" asked Mikaia.

"Because I just heard Mom say something about food!" Jonathan returned.

"Man, when it comes to food, Jonathan can hear even the slightest sound," Nicholas said to Mikaia.

"If he were a caveman he would probably even be

able to track a mouse by the sound of its whiskers against the grass!" Mikaia said. Nicholas broke into a deep belly laugh.

As they sat at the dinner table, Mikaia asked, "Were you able to get the part to fix the air conditioning unit, Dad?"

"Well, I had to change a couple of things, but Sam Hawkins did find the part I needed in his hardware store, so we have some cool air now."

"Do you know Mr. Hawkins very well?" Nicholas inquired.

"No. just from seeing him at the hardware store and of course at the school board meeting a couple of weeks ago. He seems like a rather intense sort of man, but he does know the hardware and sporting goods business," their dad, Nathan, replied.

"What have you three been up to? Did you find what you were looking for in town?"

"Not really, but we did see Mr. Peters and Jonathan bought a couple of old mining claims for his collection at the antique store," Nicholas said.

"And I treated my siblings to ice cream cones," Jonathan said proudly.

"That was very nice of you," replied their mom, Cathy.

"He was the only one with money, Mom...but I guess it was still nice of him," Mikaia said as Jonathan smiled and swallowed a rather large piece of baked potato.

After dinner and helping their mom with the dishes, the triplets headed up to Mikaia's room.

"I'm going to read through this science book and both of you should too after I'm done. It's got to hold a clue to something, and maybe together we can figure it out." said Mikaia.

"That's okay. I trust you and Nicholas with the reading. Besides I've got to get the CD and the sound system ready to go for tonight. Can we meet in this room at midnight?" Jonathan asked as he pulled Mikaia's old CD playing boom box from her closet.

"I'll be ready. Now you be careful with that old boom box, Jonathan. It's very valuable. I spotted one just like it in the antique store today," Mikaia said with a smile as Jonathan raised his eyebrows and sighed as he headed down the hall to his room.

"You know, Mikaia, with the W. Lowe's mining claim as the Essence, we could take a field trip back to sometime in 1858 and see exactly what William Lowe was up to. We might even be able to talk to him about his discoveries," Nicholas suggested.

"You're right. That flashed through my mind too when you read off his name as the owner."

"Then I hope things go well tonight and we can scare Arnold and North away so we can take a field trip," Nicholas replied.

Nicholas's alarm clock sounded at 11:45 p.m. He jumped up, put on some warm clothes, washed up quickly, and walked quietly down the hall to Mikaia's room. Both Mikaia and Jonathan were waiting.

"Man, what time did you get up?" he asked, a bit surprised that they were both ready, especially Mikaia.

"Just a few minutes ago," answered Mikaia.

"Do you both have flashlights?" Jonathan asked.

"I do," Nicholas said and Mikaia held hers up.

"I've got mine and the boom box ready for an evening serenade," Jonathan said with a smile. "Let's go, but keep it quiet. We don't want Mom and Dad to know what we're up to."

They hurried out the back and towards the creek. They knew the way by heart now and the darkened skies barely slowed them down. Within a few minutes they were working their way through the apple orchard to the bushes where Arnold and North had pitched their tent. All was quiet. The triplets found a spot behind some bushes about thirty feet away from the tent where they could move unseen from the campsite.

"This looks just right," Jonathan whispered. "We can walk the boom box back and forth behind these bushes to make it sound like the lion is moving without being seen."

"Okay, Maestro, let the music play," Nicholas suggested.

With that Jonathan turned on the boom box so the lion sounds quietly came out.

They looked to see if there was any
movement in the tent.

"That's perfect!" Mikaia whispered. "If I didn't know I was standing next to a recorded lion sound I would be out of here in a second!"

They all looked through the bushes trying to see if there was any movement in the tent.

"I think they're sound asleep, Jonathan. Turn it up a bit louder," Nicholas suggested.

Jonathan turned the volume up a little higher, but there was still no movement in the tent.

"Boy, those two must have taken sleeping pills," whispered Jonathan.

"Maybe this will help," Nicholas said as he snuck closer to the tent and picked up a couple of small dead branches. From about fifteen feet away he tossed the first stick, then the second against the tent and hurried back to the others.

After a few seconds the triplets could see a flashlight go on in the tent and heard the boys quietly talking.

"Okay, let's walk this lion back and forth a bit," Jonathan said as he started moving through the space to his left.

A second flashlight lit up inside the tent.

"I think we have their full attention now," Nicholas whispered above the growls and groans of the lion.

"What do you think they're doing?" Mikaia asked.

"Probably packing, wouldn't you be if you thought a lion was a few feet from your tent and could pounce in at any moment?" replied Jonathan.

Just then the startled triplets heard the loud clanging of cow bells when the boys jumped from their tent yelling with their flashlights pointed in the direction of the lion sound. Arnold and North appeared to be slowly walking towards them.

"What should we do?" Mikaia asked.

"Don't move," ordered Nicholas. "Jonathan, quick, turn the volume up a bit and move toward the bushes to the right which are closer to them."

"You're sure, Nicholas?"

"Yes," Nicholas returned as Jonathan increased the growling sound just when it sounded most threatening.

Then North yelled out, "No way, Arnold, I'm out of here!"

"No come back, the bells will scare it away!" Arnold yelled as he rang the bell even harder.

The triplets could see the light of a flashlight disappear down the school road towards the main highway. The other light stayed in one place for a moment. Jonathan moved back along the bushes where Nicholas picked up another branch and brushed it loudly against the bushes in front of them. Within a second or two they saw the other flashlight disappear down the road and heard the distant ringing of a cow bell.

"That was perfect!" Mikaia exclaimed. "At that speed they'll be to town in a few minutes."

"And we need to get out of here," Nicholas said as he pulled a branch off a nearby digger pine tree.

"What are you doing?" Jonathan asked.

"Covering our tracks in case they come back tomorrow and look in these bushes," he replied as he bent down and slowly walked backwards sweeping the pine needles back and forth across their foot prints.

"Nicholas, how were you so sure they would run like that if we stayed?" Jonathan asked.

"I wasn't sure about Arnold. But after meeting North and seeing his concern about lions, I figured he'd be gone in no time. With him gone, Arnold would have no choice but to run away too."

"Good job, boys!" said Mikaia. "Do you think they'll stay way?"

"Would you come back and stay another night after this?" Jonathan asked.

"Not without an army," Mikaia replied.

"Then we probably can start taking field trips soon. We'll still need to be careful. I'm sure Sam Hawkins and the others will be very unhappy when they find out the boys took off. They'll think up other ways to stop us," Nicholas replied as the triplets headed through the orchard, flashlights in hand.

The phone rang several times before it was picked up.

"Who's calling?" a stern voice asked.

"It's me, Sam."

"Why are you calling so early? It's barely six AM."

"The boys came running home late last night from the old school," Sam replied.

"They what?" the voice responded loudly. "I thought you said things were under control. You said the boys would camp and watch until school started, stopping the Frazier kids from going on field trips."

"They say their tent got attacked by a mountain lion so they took off," Sam replied.

"You know as well as I do that a lion hasn't been spotted around Opportunity since last year!" the voice replied as it grew louder.

"I know, but their description of the sounds it made add up. One could have returned," Sam said.

"Are you going to send them back?" the high-pitched voice asked.

"I don't think they will go back. Arnold would, but not alone. Since his friend North won't go, Arnold won't return either," answered Sam.

"Well I expect you to fix this or think of something else. We need to stop the trips or destroy the power of the old school," the voice said angrily.

"I'll talk to Pete and check with Phil and Mabel. I'm sure we can come up with something.

"Remember, we're not supposed to hurt the triplets, but anything else goes! Now get on it! If Cryptic has to become directly involved, you'll all be sorry," said the voice as the phone banged down.

Chapter Five

The Creekside Mine

"Pass the butter, please, Mikaia," Nicholas requested. "I want to butter these pancakes while they're still warm."

"Suurre," replied Mikaia while she was in the middle of a big yawn.

"You three seem tired today. You've hardly said anything since you sat down for breakfast," their mom observed.

"I didn't sleep well last night. I guess it was just one of those nights. Maybe the caffeine from the Mountain Dew soda kept me awake," Nicholas replied.

"I've warned you about having anything with caffeine in it in the evening," returned their mom.

"I think I had a few too many sips of Nicholas's," Jonathan added.

"I had that last piece of chocolate cake I was saving. Maybe too much chocolate kept me awake too," Mikaia replied.

"That could do it since there is a lot of caffeine in

chocolate," their mom said as she placed some more pancakes on Jonathan's plate.

"I'll wait for both of you up in my room when you're done," Mikaia said as she left the kitchen. "Thanks, Mom, for the pancakes."

"If you're making plans for the day make sure you save some time for your chores," their mom said. "As you know there is..."

"Always more to do on a ranch," Jonathan and Nicholas said together.

"At least I know you both have been listening to me," their mom replied.

"We'll get them done before we go anywhere," Nicholas said.

Up in Mikaia's room the triplets agreed to do their chores quickly and then, if the way was clear, take a field trip. However, they disagreed about where they should go.

"I still say we should go to Midst and see if we can summon Halo. Then we can find out what he knows about the power of the old school," Mikaia advised.

"But if we follow William Lowe's Essence that he left on his 1858 mining claim, we can ask the very person who put the power into the old school when he built it for the community in 1860," Jonathan argued.

"You both make sense," Nicholas interjected. "Our main goal is to discover what the power is and where its source is located so we can protect it from

Cryptic and his Followers."

"Then we'd better talk to William Lowe," urged Jonathan. "You have to remember that Halo, as the Master Inventor's guide, only tells us what we need to know to figure things out. It's like a learning program for us. He still may not tell us all he knows about the power and its source."

"That's true, Jonathan. I think we should go directly to the source and see William Lowe," Nicholas agreed breaking the tie between Jonathan and Mikaia.

"If that's what you two want to do it's all right with me. But I still think we should be getting Halo's help," Mikaia said as she walked out of her room grabbing a large pile of laundry from the hall floor.

"Then I'll pull some weeds and water Mom's plants," Nicholas said walking out behind her.

"And I'm heading into the garage to knock down all the spider webs Dad wanted cleaned up...and I don't like spiders! Last time two fell on my neck! How about us trading jobs next time, Nicholas?" Jonathan suggested.

"No way! Dad sees you as the Spiderman since you do such a great job. Just get out of their way when they're falling," Nicholas returned with a snicker.

"Thanks a lot Nicholas!" Jonathan replied, reluctantly walking towards the garage.

By mid-morning the triplets met on the front porch.

"Do you have the old school class list, Mikaia, just in case we pick up another Essence on our trip?" asked Nicholas.

"I've got it right here," she replied. "And who has the Creekside Mine Claim?"

"I have it in my pocket and I've rubbed it all over me," Jonathan answered. "And in case you're interested I even had to swat a couple of spiders off my sleeve with it."

"Just don't tear it, Jonathan," warned Mikaia.

"I'm sure a couple of squashed spiders on it won't hurt it much," Jonathan replied.

"Boys!" An exasperated Mikaia exclaimed as they headed around the back towards the creek.

As they came to the orchard Nicholas suggested they approach the old school from the playground side just behind the spot Arnold and North pitched their tent.

"The tent's still there," Mikaia said.

"They're probably still too afraid to come and get it," Jonathan said with a conquering smile.

"I'll sneak up and peek in to make sure they didn't come back," Nicholas said as he worked his way through the bushes towards the tent.

Not hearing or seeing anything, he slowly moved around to the front and peeked in. Inside he could see two unzipped sleeping bags, a couple bottles of water and a large paper bag which looked and smelled like it held a couple of old tuna sandwiches. Nicholas guessed that Evelyn Hawkins either wasn't such a good cook after all or she didn't want to waste her talents on the two boys who were just camping out. He turned around and waved for Nicholas and Mikaia to join him.

"Boy that tuna sure smells bad," Jonathan said as he peeked in.

"We'd better hit the slide or the merry-go-round right away in case someone comes back to pick this stuff up," Jonathan suggested.

"Let's use the slide to slide back in time, hopefully to 1858," Mikaia said.

"Remember, Jonathan on first, then Mikaia, then me," Nicholas reminded them. Then we lock legs, close our eyes, push off and think of Midst!" he said as they climbed up the ladder and got into position.

"Ready guys?" Mikaia inquired. When both boys nodded yes, she yelled, "Then ready, set, push!" and they quickly sped down the slide.

Just before hitting the bottom they floated into the swirling cotton candy clouds that were whirling around them. Everything was white as they dropped down onto the clouds of Midst.

"You've got visitors again, Yon!" Hither yelled out.

"Maybe it's a false alarm. Remember last week when you thought we had some time travelers but it ended up being a passing satellite?" Yon yelled back.

"Well if it's a satellite then there are three of them

and they look a lot like the triplets," Hither yelled.

"Why would anyone send up three satellites that look like the triplets?" returned Yon.

"Yon, it is the triplets. They're sitting on a cloud right next to me!"

"Are you sure it's not a satellite, I'm rather busy right now," Yon replied.

"Hi Hither," Mikaia said with a big smile and wave.

"Yon, one of the satellites just talked to me," Hither yelled.

"Silly, satellites don't talk...do they?" Yon yelled back.

"Of course not, Yon. It was Mikaia talking," Hither said in disgust.

"Wow, a satellite that looks and talks like Mikaia! I've got to see this," Yon said as he quickly approached. "Hither, what's the matter with you? They're not satellites! They're Mikaia, Nicholas, and Jonathan. How could you not recognize them?"

With that Hither covered both his ears and quickly started floating away to the furthest cloud they could see. From a distance it sounded like he was screaming.

"Oh, don't worry about Hither. You see, often even small things can bother him," Yon noted.

"We're here to travel a-ways back into the past, so we need your help for that, Yon," Nicholas shared.

"You sure will, and as always I will be very

professional and efficient about it. Are you three ready to travel?" Yon asked.

All three nodded.

"Okay then, now hold hands, close your eyes...and..."

A strong wind blew across them and electricity sparked and hissed. In their minds everything was white, then turned green, then brown. Then they all felt wet. As they each felt the moisture, they jumped up at the same time.

"Man, I'm all wet," Jonathan complained.

"Me too," Mikaia yelled.

"That's because were standing ankle deep in a river," Nicholas reported.

"A what?" asked Jonathan.

"Just look around, Jonathan," Nicholas suggested.

All around them there were men moving and kneeling down along the riverbank with large pans and shovels.

"Hey, this is my claim. If you three don't want to get shot then ya better move on right now," growled a small bearded man with skin that looked like leather.

As they looked more closely they could see he had his hand on the handle of his pistol that was partly pulled from its holster.

"We mean no harm, Mister. We're just passing through and didn't mean to trespass on your claim.

We'll be on our way right now," Mikaia quickly sputtered as she grabbed Jonathan and Nicholas and pulled them away towards the shore.

"Now you're standing on my claim!" shouted a larger man who had just dropped his gold pan and picked up a rifle.

Mikaia took one look and kept pulling the two boys further away from the river bed.

"What is this all about," Jonathan said in disbelief.

"I think we arrived sometime during the California gold rush. Hopefully somewhere in 1858," Nicholas said as he kept looking around at all the digging and panning activity.

"Hey, son, you want to help me rock my Long Tom gold dust rocker. I'll give you a quarter of any gold we find when we wash this gravel through it?" an old bent man in overalls shouted out as he spit something on the ground.

"Oh, no thank you, mister. We're just passing through," Nicholas quickly answered.

"Then if you ain't goin' to help you better be movin' on!" he shouted back.

"Quick, let's get up the hill a-ways and away from the river," Mikaia said.

When they climbed up the hill about a hundred feet, they came to a dirt road running parallel to the river. Horse drawn wagons rambled along, followed by men leading donkeys as well as other miners on foot who carried all sorts of equipment.

"Why do we always end up in the middle of a dusty mess?" Jonathan asked. "Can't Yon ever drop us down into a nice meadow?"

Nicholas stepped out onto the road and questioned an older man with long hair and a gap between his teeth who was carrying a large can on each shoulder. "Excuse me mister. Can you tell us where we are?"

The man stopped for a moment and fixed his eyes on Nicholas.

"You must be another greenhorn who came a lookin' for gold and don't know nothin' about how to get it or even where you are."

"Yes, sir, you're right. We just got here," replied Jonathan.

"Figures! You missed most of the gold layin' along the rivers and streams. Now most of us are workin' the mines to find the mother lode, where the real gold comes from. I'm haulin' these two cans of black powder I just bought to a mine now. You're just outside of the great metropolis of Opportunity, son."

"Thanks! Do you know what day and year it is?" Nicholas continued.

"Darn, you don't know nothin'! Where'd you three come from? Texas?"

"No, sir, the east coast," Nicholas said.

"If I were you I'd go back to Mommy as soon as I could. You won't last a week out here," the man said as he started to walk away. Then he stopped and turned around. "So, you'll know the week you'll probably die in, it's August 20, 1858," he yelled back as he turned and spit, then headed up the road with a laugh.

"Well, this has sure been fun so far," said Jonathan.

"At least we're in the right place at the right time," Nicholas replied. "Now we need to find someone who knows William Lowe or at least where the Creekside Mine is located."

"Try to pick someone who is rational this time, Nicholas. These guys all look like they'd shoot us for a can of beans!" Jonathan observed.

"From my reading of the mining camps, Jonathan, they did!" replied Nicholas.

"Look way over there. I see a couple of buildings. Maybe someone there can help us," Mikaia suggested.

They all started moving towards the buildings, trying to stay off the crowded road.

"Assay Office, it says," Mikaia read out.

"What is an assay?" Jonathan asked.

"It's where the miners bring their gold to have it weighed and evaluated, or assessed, to see how much it's worth," Nicholas replied.

"Why can't they just put a sign up that says 'We evaluate Gold'?" Jonathan asked.

"You've got me on that one. Makes good sense to

me," replied Nicholas as they walked in the door.

Once inside the triplets could make out a couple of men standing in the far corner. There was a man at a large desk with a weight scale in front of him. As he looked up, Mikaia spoke.

"Sorry to bother you sir. We know you must be busy, but we're looking for someone and figured you'd probably know a lot of the miners around here."

"That I do little lady. Who are you looking for?" he replied as he set his glasses down on the desk.

"A gentleman named William Lowe," she replied.

"Ain't many gentlemen around here, but Lowe? Oh yeah, the Creekside Mine.

"Yeah, I know of him. His mine's just a few miles east of town. Is he a friend of yours?"

"Sort of. Some friends told us to look him up."

"He's kind of a strange fellow. Seems like he'd rather read a book than work his mine, which is not a bad producer either. He brings a lot of gold in here. Yeah, follow this road through town and turn right at the saloon. Then walk up that road a couple of miles."

"Thanks Mister," Mikaia said and the three of them slowly backed out the door.

"I say we make a bee line for the mine," Jonathan advised. "This place is weird."

"Just a different place in time," Nicholas said as they started up the road.

About a mile along the road they began to see a few two story wooden buildings.

"This must be Opportunity," Jonathan stated.

"It sure is. Look at that sign on that brick building down the block," Mikaia said as she pointed.

"Hey, the Bank of Opportunity! We've been there. And look next to us, The Mercantile and Hardware Store! Man, this is Opportunity!" Jonathan exclaimed.

"Look, there's the saloon where we turn right," said Mikaia.

"I don't remember that place," Jonathan said.

"That's because it's the Opportunity Hotel and Restaurant now, Jonathan," Nicholas replied.

"Let's keep moving up to the mine," Nicholas suggested.

The triplets followed the road as it wound up the hill east of town.

"You know, this looks familiar," Jonathan said.

"I think it's somewhere near our ranch," Mikaia said as she looked around. "But it looks so different."

"You have to remember that this is over a hundred and sixty years before we moved here. The only things that would be the same are the hills. Just about everything else would probably have been burned, cut down, and replanted in that period of time," Nicholas stated.

"Hey, look at the sign!" Jonathan said as he pointed towards a large tree next to a dirt road that led up a small hill to their left.

"Creekside Mine, here we are," said Nicholas.

The triplets walked up the hill through a grove of elm trees mixed in with some aspens. The aspen leaves shimmered in the breeze. Just behind the trees sat a small house about a hundred feet to the right of a mine tunnel that disappeared into the ground. Two men were dumping wheelbarrows loaded with a mixture of dirt and quartz near the opening, creating a large pile. The triplets approached the front door and knocked.

A tall older man in a wrinkled dark suit with a vest opened the door. He was wearing glasses and holding a book open across his palm.

"What may I do for you? Did you come for a job? We could use some more tunnelers," he said.

"Oh, no sir," Nicholas said. "We're looking for William Lowe."

"Are you friends or relatives of his?" he asked.

"We're friends of a friend," Nicholas replied.

"I'm sorry but he's gone to Mariposa for supplies. Probably back sometime tomorrow."

"We won't be here tomorrow," Jonathan said.

"You must be in a big hurry then," he replied. "I'm D.C. Powers his partner in the Creekside Mine. Maybe I can help you."

Nicholas and Mikaia looked at each other and Jonathan's mouth dropped open. They remembered that D.C. Power's name was also on the mine claim with William Lowe's. It was his Essence they had followed!

"Well, yes, you probably can help. Do you know much about science?" she asked not knowing how else to get the information they were after.

"Why yes. I have a degree in science from one of the best colleges in the east."

"Have you studied much about magnets?" Mikaia continued.

"I focused on earth science and on magnetic and electric energy," Mr. Powers replied with a puzzled look on his face. "How do you know so much to ask these questions?"

"May I ask one more question, a question that may seem even stranger?" Mikaia asked.

"You might as well, I already feel like I'm an open book," he replied.

"As a scientist, do you believe it is possible to time travel?" Mikaia asked as she looked him straight in the eye.

The book he was holding fell to the ground as an expression of disbelief and fear moved across his face. He was obviously shaken by the question and before the triplets knew it the door quickly shut.

"I guess we're not going to be able to find out much on this trip," Jonathan said as he looked over at a surprised Mikaia.

"What did you expect," Nicholas said. "He obviously knows something about it or he would have responded with laughter instead of slamming the door in our faces. So we did learn something,"

Nicholas reasoned.

"What should we do now?" asked Jonathan.

"I'm not sure, but it makes that chapter in the teacher's science book marked by the mining claim even more important," Mikaia said. "The whole chapter was about magnets, electricity and how to use them to create some kind of motor power."

Suddenly the door opened a crack. Mr. Powers peered out through his glasses as though he was examining a tiny object.

"Who are you three?" he asked.

"We can't say much right now except that we know a friend of Mr. Lowe who sent us to get some information," replied Mikaia.

The door opened even further as he slowly came out.

"I'm really curious about all this. Maybe we could talk for a moment. Why don't you have a seat," Mr. Powers said as he pointed to a bench and a couple of wooden chairs that sat on the small porch.

"Now what is this about time travel?" he asked looking at Mikaia.

"Well we've studied the idea a little and believe it is possible. That's what we came to talk to Mr. Lowe about. We heard that he feels it's possible too," Mikaia replied.

"How do you know so much at such a young age? Most educated adults think it is a crazy idea," he noted, obviously trying to figure out what they were up to.

"We're not sure how it can be done, but some kind of magnetic attraction might be involved," Nicholas added.

Mr. Power's glasses dropped further down his nose as he sat for a moment looking at them.

"There is that possibility, but in order to move through time you would have to travel at a tremendous speed, almost as fast as light, which of course is impossible."

"Is it?" Nicholas returned. The question obviously made Mr. Powers uncomfortable.

"Do you know what Mr. Lowe studied in college?" asked Mikaia.

"Uh, yes, he studied science too...How did you know he went to college?" he asked.

"The friend of a friend told us," Mikaia replied.

"Oh yes, that friend," he said as he appeared a little less cautious.

"And what was Mr. Lowe's main area of science?" Nicholas asked.

"His science specialty? He studied physics and examined light and its movement around objects. Because of our knowledge of the earth and science, we were able to discover this very profitable mine," he said with a slight smile.

"Are there many mines around here?" asked Jonathan.

"Yes, many, with miles of tunnels. It seems

everyone wants to strike it rich," he said.

"Has anyone thought about building a school? It looks like some families are starting to move into the area," Nicholas asked.

"Again, it is strange that you would ask. Since our mine has been doing so well, William and I have talked about building one someday and donating it to the town. Education is important to both of us," replied Mr. Powers.

"Do you know where you'd build it?" Jonathan quickly asked.

"You three children surely have a lot of questions," Mr. Powers said, looking like he wasn't planning to respond. "Well, if we do, we are not sure, probably some place right around here."

The triplets gave each other a quick glance. Then Mikaia spoke. "We certainly hope you build that school, and then children like us would be able to get an education."

"Speaking of children like you, just who are you?" Mr. Powers asked more determined than ever to get a response.

"Actually, we're the Frazier triplets. I'm Mikaia and these are my brothers Nicholas and Jonathan."

"Do you live around here?"

"Yes, you could say that," Nicholas replied.

"Then just what friend told you to find Mr. Lowe?"

"It was a distant relative of his, Harold Lowe,"

answered Mikaia.

"Harold Lowe? William never spoke of a Harold Lowe. Well maybe if he is a distant relative he…"

"You know, Mr. Powers," Nicholas cut in. "We need to get going now. Our parents will be wondering where we are."

"Okay, I'll let William know you came by. I am sure he will be sorry he missed you."

"We do appreciate you taking the time to talk to us," replied Jonathan.

"Yes, and we hope you do share our conversation," Nicholas added as he stood up and started down the two porch steps with Mikaia and Jonathan close behind.

The triplets walked along the short dirt road towards the one they'd followed from town.

"Wow, that was interesting," Jonathan said. "But I didn't think we were going to tell him who we were."

"I wasn't planning on it until Mikaia gave him our actual names. Then I figured out what she was doing," replied Nicholas.

"I felt that if we told the truth, Mr. Powers might share our conversation with William. Then if he actually does have a way of creating time travel in 1858 he might figure things out," added Mikaia.

"That's when I decided to help," Nicholas said.

"I missed seeing that one, but I did find out that when he does build the school he, and I guess Mr. Powers, will use some kind of magnetic energy, electricity, and light to make something happen," Jonathan replied.

"Yeah, that's the main thing we learned," Mikaia shared.

"Now we just have to figure out exactly what that power is and where it is," Nicholas added as they walked down the road towards town.

Chapter Six

Snatched

Looking down the road the triplets could see someone driving a wagon towards them.

"I suggest that now is probably a good time to go back home," Nicholas said as the man came closer.

"Let's step off the road and back into those bushes and get out of here," Mikaia replied as she made a quick right turn into some Manzanita bushes and short pines closely followed by her brothers.

"Okay, let's hold hands, close our eyes, and concentrate on where we were, and what we were thinking when we slid down the slide," Mikaia said as she took Nicholas's hand and he grabbed Jonathan's.

Just at that instant they heard a loud voice yell out, "You don't think you're getting away that easily do you. Cryptic has Followers even in 1858 you fools," they all heard as they opened their eyes and caught a glimpse of the long-haired man with a gap between his teeth. He grabbed Jonathan whose hand pulled loose from Nicholas's.

The white cotton candy cloud began to swirl

around them as they suddenly landed at their desks.

"Nicholas! Are you all right!" yelled Mikaia anxiously.

"Yes, but Jonathan pulled free from my hand just as we heard the man yell!"

They both looked quickly over at Jonathan's desk and saw that it was empty.

"Welcome back! Where is Jonathan? I thought he went with you?" Tique asked when she saw that he wasn't at his desk.

"He did!" Mikaia yelled. "But he was grabbed at the last minute by somebody who snuck up on us when we were trying to return!"

"Oh, that's terrible. I've never had that happen before!"

"What should we do, Tique?"

"I don't really know, Nicholas. I guess you'll need to go back and rescue him if you can. I remember Halo saying that it would be best if you all traveled together."

"Yeah, but how do we find our way back?" asked an anxious Mikaia.

"I'm not sure. That sounds like a good question for Halo," Tique replied.

"Nicholas, do you have the Creekside Mining claim?" Mikaia asked.

"No! Don't you?"

"No! Then Jonathan still must have it," Mikaia replied in frustration.

"What are we going to do? We need to get back to him as soon as we can. We don't know what will happen to him or what that man might do to him," Nicholas said angrily.

"Didn't I hear him say something about Cryptic?" Mikaia asked.

"Yeah, I heard it too," Nicholas replied. "He said 'Cryptic has Followers in 1858, you fools!'"

"I can't believe it! Cryptic must have known where we traveled and had one of his Followers track us down in 1858," Mikaia said, shaking her head in disbelief.

"Unfortunately, evil has no time boundaries," Tique said quietly.

"Then he knows where we're going, but not why we're going or what exactly we learn from our trips," Nicholas reasoned.

"We really need to be careful," Mikaia added. "Right now we have to find Jonathan!"

"Okay, let's think!" Nicholas said as he sat back down in his desk

There was a popping noise and Halo suddenly stood next to Tique in the front of the classroom.

"I thought I'd call Halo," Tique said. "I hope you don't mind me helping a bit. I figured this wasn't the time to review what you learned on this field trip. It's critical to find Jonathan."

"Thanks, Tique!" Nicholas said, looking over at Halo who was still wearing old jeans and a red and blue flannel shirt.

"This certainly caught me off guard," Halo said as he shook his head in disgust.

"I knew Cryptic's Followers couldn't hurt you but I never thought he'd have one of them grab one of you, especially in the past! Come to think of it, that is a good time to disrupt your use of power. He can hold one of you in time so your powers can't be joined and you can't time travel as easily."

"What are we going to do, Halo?" asked Mikaia.

"You need to find a way to get Jonathan back as soon as possible."

"Can't you help us?" Nicholas asked.

"I'm allowed to give you some information, but the Master Inventor won't allow me to do more. He has faith that you will find a way. He knows this experience will make all three of you stronger in your ability to believe in yourselves and in the powers he's allowed you to have and use."

"Then what exactly can you share with us?" Mikaia quickly asked.

"In 1858 you need to find a man named Ned Steward. He's the one who snatched Jonathan. Find Ned and you'll find Jonathan!" Halo replied.

"That's great, but how do we get back? Jonathan has the mining claim with the Essence of William Lowe and D.C. Powers on it! Without that we can't travel back to that exact time," Nicholas exclaimed.

"The Master Inventor trusts in the three of you,

Nicholas. You need to have more faith in him," Halo said softly with a slight smile.

"Yes, we know what He's done for us. He's allowed us to learn and grow and for that we're very thankful," Nicholas said quietly. "But right now, we're really concerned about Jonathan. We have to do something!"

"Nicholas!" Mikaia said

"What?" replied Nicholas.

"Steward!" Mikaia said. "Isn't that the last name of two of Cryptic's Followers in Opportunity?"

"Yeah, Phil and Mable! Mr. Peters talked about them when we saw him in town the day we visited the antique store. You don't mean that Ned is..."

"Now you're thinking. Yes," Halo said, "Ned is Phil's Grandfather! Unfortunately, Cryptic's evil does run in some families. Even through time and through Cryptic, they can work evil."

"I can't believe how these people are all tied together in some way. Seeing this happen must really sadden the Master Inventor," Mikaia replied.

"Yes, it saddens all of us who believe in goodness and love," Halo said.

"Mikaia, in town we talked to Mr. Peters, then went to the antique store. Do you remember that Jonathan and I saw another mining claim with D.C. Power's name on it?"

"Yes, you said something about it when we were planning our field trip to find William Lowe."

"That's the key! We've got to get back to the antique store right away and hope no one has purchased that old mining claim!" Nicholas exclaimed as he hurried towards the door with Mikaia right behind him.

"Thanks for the help!" Mikaia yelled as they disappeared through the door.

"Class dismissed!" Tique announced.

"Do you remember what claim it was, Nicholas?" Mikaia asked.

"I remember it was the Timber something Mining Claim, but I can't remember the date on it!"

"I sure hope it was close to August 20, 1858, like the Creekside claim. If not, we might have to wait for several months or years to pass in Opportunity during the gold rush until it becomes August 20th and we can stop Jonathan from being snatched!"

"That would be miserable, even though back home they'd only think we'd been gone for a couple of hours once we came back! Now that's really weird," Nicholas replied.

When Nicholas and Mikaia arrived at the house, they found a note on the kitchen table from their mom that said she and their dad had driven to town to pick up some food for dinner.

"Darn!" said Nicholas. "There goes our quick trip to town."

"Well there are always our bikes," Mikaia said with a smile.

"We haven't used them much since we got here because we're always hiking through the woods to the old school. I think we'd make good time into town on them."

"And not so good time riding back up from town to the old school!" Mikaia replied.

"Why don't you go check them out and I'll grab our bike helmets and leave a note for Mom and Dad."

"Sounds like a plan. We'll meet in the garage," Nicholas said, running towards the garage. "And don't forget to grab some money too," he yelled as Mikaia waved and dashed into the house.

The bike trip down the winding road to town only took them sixteen minutes.

They parked their bikes in front of the antique store just as a tall lady walked out the door.

"Oh, hi! How are the two of you? Are you still tracing back the family histories of the students that attended the old school from the class lists I gave you?" the lady asked"

"How'd you know? Oh, I'm sorry. I remember you," Mikaia quickly said. "You're from the Foothill Unified School District Office."

"Hi," Nicholas said. "You're Miss Ivy, the Administrative Assistant to the Superintendent. You helped us register for school!"

"Yes, what good memories you two have. I don't see your brother. Is he all right?"

"Oh yes, he just couldn't ride into town with us.

He got hung up in something he had to do," replied Nicholas.

"And yes, we are still researching the family histories of the students who attended the old school from the class lists you copied for us...thanks," Mikaia replied with a smile.

"You're welcome, and I hope your brother can get into town soon...I'd like to see him again too," Miss Ivy said as she turned and walked away.

"Quick, let's get inside and grab that mining claim," Nicholas said as he flung open the door and moved to the documents section and grabbed a stack of old mining claims.

"It's nice to see you again!" a familiar voice said.

"Hi, Terry. We just had to come back and look over your old mining claims again...Jonathan, our brother really liked the two he bought the other day, so we thought we'd buy him another for a gift," Nicholas said as he and Mikaia thumbed through a second stack.

"Well those old claims seem to have become a hot item," Terry said.

Nicholas and Mikaia both looked up.

"What do you mean?" asked Mikaia.

"That lady, Miss Ivy, who was just in here spent twenty minutes looking through them. She said she was looking for one she needed to get some background information for the Superintendent. But I can't for the life of me figure out why she'd need an old claim from the Timber Pine Mine."

Nicholas and Mikaia froze. Neither could respond for a moment as they turned and looked up at Terry in bewilderment.

"Did you say the Timber Pine Mining Claim?" Mikaia finally asked.

"Yes, that's the one."

As he almost choked, Nicholas asked, "Did she buy it?"

"Oh, no, she looked for a long time but couldn't find it. I told her I don't remember selling one by that name," Terry said, as Nicholas sighed loudly.

"Don't tell me that's the one you're looking for too?"

"Actually, yes, Jonathan saw it here the other day and really wanted it, but he only had enough money for two," Nicholas replied.

"Well I'll be. If he saw it here the other day then it's got to be here somewhere," Terry said. "Spend as much time looking as you like," she said, walking back over to the counter.

"Now that is really weird," Mikaia quietly said to Nicholas. "What's going on here?"

"I don't know but we have to find that claim."

They looked twice through the two stacks of claims but couldn't find the Timber Pines. Suddenly Nicholas's eyes lit up and he got this strange look on his face.

"What's the matter?"

"It's great to be a bit careless sometimes," he said as he bent down to the shelf below.

"What do you mean?" Mikaia asked.

"I remember now that I had the Timber Pine claim in my hand when I bent down to look through the stack of old land deeds on the second shelf. I don't remember placing it back with the other mining claims. So, I must have laid it back down with the land deeds...and yep, here it is!" he said with a big smile.

"Quick, read it! What does it say?" Mikaia almost ordered.

"The Timber Pines Mining Claim, filed by D.C. Powers on August 20, 1858! Man, what luck! They filed this claim on the same day as the Creekside claim!" Nicholas enthusiastically replied.

"Let's buy it right away and get out of here. Someone else may be looking for this," Mikaia said.

"Oh, you found it. Well then, it's yours for five dollars," Terry said seeming a little surprised as Mikaia quickly handed over a five-dollar bill.

"Plus tax," Terry returned. "We've got to pay Uncle Sam."

Fortunately, Mikaia had brought another dollar as she paid the tax and they ran out the door.

The ride back up into the hills seemed to take forever, but they finally arrived at the old school.

After placing their bikes against the porch, Mikaia and Nicholas ran to the slide.

Chapter Seven

Ned Steward

Ned Steward glared at Jonathan. "And you three thought you had everythin' figured out," the long-haired man with a gap between his teeth snarled. "You're so uppity that you think Cryptic's Followers are stupid! He knows what you've been up to and let me know. He even knew where and when you'd be landin'. All I had to do is hang out there 'til I saw you three drop in. As long as I keep you hidden, your brother and sister won't be able to time travel. Heck, they won't even be able to get back here since I found the Creekside Minin' Claim you used in your pocket. It was torn up a bit, but now they can't come to help you! Isn't that just dandy? Ha, Ha, Ha!"

All Jonathan could do was sit there. His hands were still tied in front, and his feet were tied around his ankles. At least the man had taken off the canvas bag he'd thrown over his head when he grabbed him. Jonathan's heart was still pounding from the surprise as he looked around the darkened cave in which he'd been placed. He had felt every bump on the road from the wagon ride to wherever the man had taken him. It wasn't very far from where all three of them had been. He figured maybe two to three miles away. He hoped that Nicholas and Mikaia had gotten home all right and had at least seen the man who'd snatched him.

"So, what do you plan on doing with me, Mister?" Jonathan cautiously asked.

"You might as well call me 'Ned' 'cause you'll be seeing a lot of me for a looong time," he said with a laugh. "Why you might sit here 'til you're all grow'd up and have a long beard a hangin' down."

"They'll find me, Ned. If they have any trouble they can always count on help from Halo and the Master Inventor."

"Shoot! Do you think that the Master Inventor has time for this kind of thing? And Halo, he may find out who snatched you but he don't have the power to know where I've hidden you. No, you're mine for a while, or 'til Cryptic gets tired of you."

"You know you can't hurt me, unless I become a Follower too!"

"Boy, there are lots a-things that can happen to a man besides just pain! Now you think about that. I've got some business to attend to. And don't get any ideas about gettin' out of here. Up the cave a-ways there's a twelve-foot-long hole across the ground that drops off a hundred feet down to another cave level, and I'll have the boards I use to get across pulled over to the other side. Now I'll see you for breakfast, or maybe lunch, or maybe I'll just toss some food over after dinner. Darn, I'm going to have a lot of fun!" Ned said as he disappeared around the corner.

"Nicholas, you go up the slide first and I'll put my legs around you," Mikaia suggested.

"Okay," replied Nicholas. "Do you see anyone around?"

"No! I looked around as we were riding up and running over to the slide."

"Me too!" said Nicholas.

"Do you have the Timber Pine Mining Claim?" asked Mikaia.

"In my front pocket."

"Then let's go! On ready, set, go! Think about Midst!" Mikaia yelled as they pushed off and slid rapidly down the slide. Like Jonathan had done, Nicholas straightened his legs out getting ready in case they hit the sand. He felt a sharp jolt to his body as the sand smashed into his face.

"Man, that smarts!" Nicholas said as he rolled over in the sand at the base of the slide with Mikaia landing on top of him.

"What happened?" Mikaia asked, quickly standing up.

"I don't know. I do remember Halo telling us that we should travel together to be sure everything goes well. Now I see what he meant," Nicholas said as he spit out some sand.

"Yes, but he never said we couldn't travel alone," Mikaia replied. "He said that each of us possesses the three traits that a child needs to be selected for field trips!"

"Let's see, the traits are: a curious mind, which Halo said you possess the most of; an adventurous heart, which Jonathan has the most of; and a caring soul, which Halo said I have the most of. So, since Jonathan isn't here, maybe we're missing an adventurous heart!"

"What do you mean? Jonathan got snatched from us in 1858 and we're risking being stuck there too if things go wrong! Not counting all the other risky field trips we've been on, we don't have enough adventure in our hearts? I don't think so!"

"Well, I agree with you. I say we try again and think of Midst and all our adventures as we slip down the slide!" Nicholas concluded, climbing back up to the top with Mikaia behind him.

"Okay, now think hard about our adventures and Midst. On ready, set, go!" yelled Mikaia.

Again, they pushed off and rapidly moved down the slide. Nicholas put his legs out and closed his eyes and mouth hoping not to get too big a jolt or too much sand in his face. Much to their pleasant surprise when they hit the bottom they just floated into the swirling white cotton candy and felt themselves softly land on the clouds of Midst.

"Man, I'm glad we didn't crash again," Nicholas said.

"And I'm glad it worked!" replied Mikaia.

"And I'm also glad you made it," they heard Halo's voice say.

"Halo, what are you doing here?" asked Mikaia.

"We knew you two would find a way to get back to your brother," Halo replied.

"Yes, Halo came to observe how well we do our job," Yon interjected.

"He didn't come to observe us, Yon. He came to give Nicholas and Mikaia some more information that might help them find Jonathan," Hither shared.

"Isn't Halo going to watch as I send them back in time to 1858?" asked Yon.

"I imagine so, if he's still here when you send them," replied Hither.

"Then I was right!"

"What do you mean you were right?" Hither sputtered back.

"Halo will observe me doing a professional and efficient job when I send them on."

"Yon, you're missing the whole point, Halo..."

"Hither, let me take it from here," Halo said as he raised his hand. "As I told you earlier, a man named Ned Steward has Jonathan. Cryptic is somehow able to track you when you take field trips with just enough time to get his Followers moving. I don't know how he does it, but it's one more thing you need to plan for. Now he knows you're coming back so I'm sure he's told Ned to hide Jonathan somewhere that's very hard to find."

"We'll find him!" Mikaia exclaimed now more determined than ever.

"To help you I've asked Yon to send you back to just a few moments after Jonathan was taken. If we try to get you any closer in time you may be harmed by bumping into your other selves," Halo said. "Okay, Yon, it's time for them to go."

"Thanks again, Halo," Nicholas said.

"Good! I'm on! See Hither, Halo is going to observe me doing my job!" Yon yelled.

"Now hold hands, close your eyes and..."

Mikaia and Nicholas felt a strong wind blow across them and again heard electricity sparking and hissing. In their minds everything was white. Then they saw green leaves above them as they found themselves lying in the road just above the turn-off to the Creekside Mine.

"This must be just after Ned grabbed Jonathan," Nicholas reasoned.

"Hey, look to the east, up the road. Do you see a wagon turning around that bend to the right?" Mikaia asked.

"That's what it looks like to me through all the dust," Nicholas replied.

"Look at those signs on the tree up a-ways," Mikaia said as she started walking towards them.

"This must be the tree all the miners use! The Tunnel Mine, the Johnston Mine, the Hole in the Mountain Mine, The Strike It Rich Mine and the Timber Pine Mine, all have arrows pointing up this road!" Nicholas reported.

"At least we know which direction it is to the Timber Pine Mine. Shall we go?" asked Mikaia.

"Wait! We just used that mine and D.C. Powers Essence on the mining claim to get us back here. Remember, D.C. Powers right now is at the Creekside Mine. We need to see him again to find out what he knows about Ned Steward and where we can find him."

"You're right, Nicholas. Let's see if he'll open the door again," Mikaia replied.

They both walked down the road until they came to the sign that pointed up to the Creekside Mine. They paused for a moment, both knowing how important it was to find Jonathan and get the information they needed from Mr. Powers. They noticed that men were still piling wheelbarrows full of quartz and dirt in front of the mine. Mikaia and Nicholas walked up the two steps and knocked on the door. They heard a voice inside mumbling something about how a man can't get anything done with all this door knocking. Mr. Powers slowly opened the door and peeked out.

"Mr. Powers, it's just us again, the Fraziers," Mikaia said trying to peer back at him through the crack.

"Didn't you three just leave a few minutes ago?" he asked as he opened the door a bit more.

"Yes, we did, and we're sorry we had to come back and bother you again, but we had one more question," Mikaia continued.

"I thought there were three of you. Where is the other boy...Jonathan I think?"

"Jonathan's waiting for us," Nicholas quickly answered.

"Then what is your question?" asked Mr. Powers.

"Do you know a man named Ned Steward and if so could you tell us how to find him?" Mikaia asked.

"That claim jumping bushwhacker! He is the last man anyone would want to see. If you see him coming, you hide all your valuables and chain your horses to a tree! What do you need to see him for?"

"He has something of ours we need to get back," Mikaia said.

"He's probably got something of everybody," Mr. Powers said angrily. "You've got to watch that man. He can be mean. But if you really want to chance it, I know where he usually hides out. I followed him one night about two weeks ago after we lost a good wheelbarrow. Try the Tunnel Mine just up the road. Unfortunately, it's near another mining claim I have up there."

"Is that the Timber Pine Mine?" asked Nicholas.

"Where do you children get all your information?

Few people know I have a claim on that mine...Yeah, I know, the friend of William Lowe told you."

"We really appreciate your help, and be sure to tell Mr. Lowe we were here when he comes back tomorrow," Mikaia said as she and Nicholas hurried away.

"Sounds like Ned Steward is a pretty popular guy around here," Mikaia said.

"Yeah, the worst of the worst, figures! We'll have to be very careful," Nicholas replied.

"Let's head on up and poke around a bit," suggested Mikaia.

"Okay, but first I want to go down the road a-ways where Jonathan was grabbed."

"Why there? We already know where Ned probably hangs out," asked Mikaia.

"Let's just say these dirt roads are like a road map. Maybe it can shed some light on where Ned might have dragged Jonathan."

"Good point," Mikaia responded as they walked down the road to the bushes and trees they had just stood in when they traveled back home.

"Look! Here are our prints in the bushes and here's where a set of boots come in right next to Jonathan. You can see where Jonathan tried to fight back but Ned must have somehow tied Jonathan up quickly."

"I see a fresh set of wagon tracks, Nicholas. This must be where he stopped. There are two sets of footprints right next to the wheel marks. One must be Jonathan's.

"And that was probably the wagon we saw heading up the hill when we got here a few minutes ago," Nicholas observed. "Now let's follow these wagon tracks up the hill and see where they lead us."

They followed the wagon tracks as they wound up the road, first to the right then to the left, passing the turn-off to the Johnston Mine and the Hole-In the-Mountain Mine.

"Just a second, Mikaia," said Nicholas as he bent down and picked up something from the road.

"What is that?"

"It looks like a small piece of brown paper. It must have been dropped recently or the dirt and weather would have destroyed it," Nicholas replied. They kept walking up the road passing the Strike It Rich Mine turn off.

There Nicholas reached down again and picked up another torn piece of brown paper from the road.

"That's funny. These two pieces fit together. They were torn off the same piece of paper," said Nicholas.

The road took a sharp turn south, crossed a small creek, then went up a hill and looped slightly to the west. About a half mile further they came to the turnoff to the Timber Pine Mine.

"This place looks familiar too," Nicholas said.

"Here's the claim you have in your pocket, Nicholas," Mikaia said. "It's the other one that Mr.

Powers owns."

"Looks like the Tunnel Mine is the last one up this road. Just our luck, it couldn't have been the first one. Speaking of luck, look, here's another brown piece of torn paper. It fits with the other two and has two letters on it...a 't' and a 'y'," Nicholas said with a puzzled expression.

"Nicholas!" shouted Mikaia. "Let me see the Timber Pines Mining claim you have in your pocket."

Nicholas quickly pulled it out and unfolded it.

"Look, it's the same kind of paper! And look at the right side on the very bottom. It says 'filed in Mariposa County'!" Mikaia said as she pointed.

"I got it!" Nicholas said as he matched the three brown torn pieces to the bottom corner next to the 't' and 'y' in county.

"It matches!" yelled Mikaia.

"That Jonathan is amazing! He's left us a paper trail with pieces from the Creekside Mining claim he had in his pocket! Now all we have to do is collect pieces of paper!" Nicholas said with a big smile.

They hiked further up the hill finding another piece of brown paper about a half a block up the dirt road as it turned south-east.

When they arrived at the turn-off to The Tunnel Mine they found two pieces of paper right where the wagon tracks turned in and headed up a smaller dirt road. About a hundred feet further they found another. That went on for another two hundred yards until they could see a wagon and a shack next to a tunnel heading into a hill. By now it was starting to get dark.

"We don't have much time to poke around or even be able to see the paper trail," said Nicholas. "Jonathan could be in the shack or the mine. We can't afford to follow any more of the paper trail up the road where we could be seen from the shack."

"Then why don't you sneak through those trees to the shack and peek in the window. If you see Jonathan inside, point your finger towards the window. If you see Ned inside and he's not paying attention, point towards the mine and I'll follow the paper trail up the road," Mikaia suggested.

"I'm on my way," Nicholas said as he crept through the trees and around to the corner of the shack. He crawled over to the front side window and carefully looked in. He could see a lantern burning and a man with long hair sitting at a table with his back to the window. Nicholas realized it must be Ned. He couldn't see anyone else. He pointed towards the tunnel as Mikaia made her way along the road looking for more paper. About every twenty feet he saw her bend down and pick something up until she was right in front of the tunnel. From there she stepped into some bushes to the left of the tunnel. Nicholas snuck around and joined her.

"Look, I've got about ten more pieces of the mining claim with the last one right in front of the mine. He's got to be in there, Nicholas."

"Let's go in. Ned looked busy with something he was working on at the table," Nicholas said. He reached down and picked up a couple of boards about five feet long and handed one to Mikaia.

"What are these for?" she asked.

"If it gets too dark in there, we may have to feel our way through," Nicholas said as he started into the dimly lit tunnel.

The cave gradually got darker as they worked their way in about fifty feet. When they turned a corner, they could see some light reflecting off of the walls about thirty feet further.

Suddenly Nicholas pushed his board forward and felt nothing. He quickly grabbed Mikaia and yelled at her to stop. There below them was a deep, dark shaft going straight down.

"Thanks, Nicholas," Mikaia said. "You must have been reaching out further with your board than I was. One more step and I would have fallen into that hole!"

"Hey, is that you, Ned?" a familiar voice asked.

"Jonathan, is that you?" Mikaia responded.

"Hi you guys. What took you so long? This cave is the pits!" Jonathan said. They could see his shadowed form just on the other side of the wide hole.

"How are you doing?" asked Nicholas.

"Better now that I've got the ropes off my arms and legs, but I can't figure out a way to get across the hole. Ned said there were long boards that he used to get across. Do you see them?" Jonathan asked.

"Yeah, I just bumped into them piled along the wall to my right," Nicholas said. "They look like they're about fifteen feet long, but they're thick, so they should hold some weight."

"Well shove a couple over, I want out of here!" Jonathan said.

"By the way, Jonathan, nice paper trail," said Nicholas.

"I thought you'd find that, if you made it back. I'm sure glad Ned tied my hands in front so I could reach into my pocket for the claim," Jonathan replied.

Nicholas and Mikaia pushed one of the heavy boards closer to the shaft. As they tried to push it out and over the wide hole, the board started to dip into the shaft. They both grunted as they used all their strength to stop it from falling in.

"I wonder how he got these things to lay across the hole? We can't tilt them up then drop them over since the tunnel isn't high enough," Nicholas said.

"I've got an idea," Jonathan said as he disappeared around the corner for a moment and came back with something in his hands.

"What did you find?" asked Mikaia.

"The ropes I took off my hands and legs. If I tie them together I'll only have about ten feet, but if I make a loop on the end and you push the board out as far as you can, maybe I can lasso it and pull it over,"

Jonathan replied.

"Great idea," Nicholas said as he and Mikaia pushed another board out about eight feet over the hole. They had weighted it down so it wouldn't fall in.

"Ride 'em cowboy," Jonathan exclaimed as he swung the rope around his head then let it go towards the end of the board.

"Darn, I think that doggie got away," he said. "I'll try again."

"You're sure in a good mood for someone stuck on the wrong side of a wide shaft," Nicholas said.

"Well a few minutes ago I was looking forward to growing old in this damp hole. Now I've got a chance to get out," he replied.

"I get your point," Nicholas said. "We'll try to bring the end up a bit to make it easier to slip on the rope."

Jonathan swung the rope around his head several more times while concentrating on the end of the board. Then he let go.

"That little doggie is coming home to me!" he said as the loop tightened around the board and he began to pull the next seven feet of board over to the edge of the shaft.

After centering the board across the hole, Jonathan carefully put some weight on it.

"Looks like it might hold okay. After all Ned got across on it and he weighs more than me," he said. He slowly worked his way across the board as both

Mikaia and Nicholas held their breaths.

After about twenty seconds of the greatest balancing act of Jonathan's life, he was across. Mikaia was the first to hug him, then Nicholas who said, "Great balance, Jonathan. Good to see you."

"Now we can get out of here," said Mikaia. "Quick, let's all hold hands and..."

"Where do you think you're goin'? They told me you two was on your way. You three ain't goin' to get away from me and make a fool out of me again. I don't care what Cryptic says. I think all of you belong in that hole," Ned, now in a rage, yelled as he swung a board at the triplets trying to knock them into the shaft.

"You're not supposed to be able to hurt us!" Mikaia yelled as they backed up right next to the deep hole.

"Well let's just see!" he yelled as he charged forward using the board like a bulldozer to push them into the shaft.

"Think Midst!" was all Mikaia had time to say when they saw Ned charge forward into the empty space where they once stood and fall forward into the shaft. They felt a strong wind blowing across them and heard electricity sparking and hissing. White cotton candy swirled around them. Then everything was white as they gently lowered onto a cloud.

It was completely quiet except for the sound of their beating hearts. Jonathan was the first to speak up. "I never thought I'd be this happy to be sitting on a cloud again!"

"Well we're glad you made it back to Midst too. You had us all worried there for a while," Hither said.

"I wasn't worried at all. I knew they could take care of themselves. I had faith, just like Halo said," replied Yon.

"Yes, we're all glad you were able to find Jonathan and get back safely," Halo said.

"Halo, how did we get here and not back to the old school?" Nicholas asked.

"At the last moment Mikaia yelled out for you to think of Midst. So, with a little help from me, we brought you back here," Halo said with a smile.

"I think Ned Steward fell into the shaft when he tried to push us in, Halo," Mikaia said sadly.

"Yes, Mikaia, I'm afraid he did. The Master Inventor grieves at any loss of life that he has created, even those who turn to Cryptic and evil. It wasn't your fault so don't blame yourselves."

"But why do people turn to evil?" asked Mikaia.

"Remember, Mikaia, besides our soul, which is the most important part of us given by the Master Inventor, He gives us our individual Essence. Our Essence makes us each different and special. We absorb a bit of this Essence from each other and the places others have been or things they have touched. That is what you follow when you time travel on field trips. That is why it is important to love and care about others instead of doing harm. Others will be better or worse people depending on whom they associate with," Halo explained.

"We know that most people are good and have love in their hearts and a caring soul or at least try to be that way," Nicholas replied. "But why do they turn to Cryptic and become like Ned Steward?"

"Often people become selfish and consider only their own needs and wants. Soon they lose their sense of goodness which gave them strong morals and values and concern for others. For them it gradually becomes easier to focus only on their own wants. They begin to make poor decisions. To justify their poor behavior and make themselves feel better, they try to get others to agree with them."

"So they turn others into selfish people?" Jonathan asked.

"Yes, soon good and evil no longer exist in their minds. They no longer turn to the Master Inventor who is love and goodness, but to Cryptic who encourages them to continue their evil ways. That is when he gets them as his Followers."

"I find that very sad, Halo," Jonathan said.

"It is, Jonathan. That's why it's so important to be careful of choices that don't feel right, or decisions that may have harmful effects on others. If we don't, Cryptic's Followers break us down."

"Halo, something strange happened to us when we went to the antique shop to buy the Timber Pine

Mining Claim of Mr. Powers. Miss Ivy was there before us looking for the same mining claim. Terry, the owner, told us that Miss Ivy said she was doing some research for her boss the School Superintendent," Nicholas said.

"That is an unusual coincidence. I don't know her as a Follower or the Superintendent either. It does suggest we need to watch them. If she had bought the mining claim, you probably wouldn't have been able to go back and rescue Jonathan. It seems Cryptic's knowledge and powers may be growing."

"If Cryptic can follow us, even through time, and let his Followers know where we are, our field trips will become even more dangerous, won't they?" asked Mikaia.

"I'm afraid you are right. He is really trying hard to stop you and destroy your powers. What he doesn't know is that your powers are growing too," Halo replied.

"What do you mean?" Jonathan asked.

"The Master Inventor is so pleased with the three of you that he has given you more powers to help you learn and to use them to do good."

"What kind of powers?" Jonathan asked.

"You will find them when you need them," Halo answered with a smile.

"That doesn't help much," Jonathan replied.

"So far hasn't everything turned out the way you had hoped?" asked Halo.

"Yes, we know. We just have to have faith," Jonathan returned.

"See, you already know the source of your true power," Halo said as he disappeared with a popping noise.

"Man, why doesn't he just tell us these things?" Jonathan muttered.

"Because we're supposed to learn them by ourselves, that's why," Mikaia replied.

"Speaking of learning, you three need to go to school. Tique is waiting for you," advised Hither.

"And I'm ready to send them," Yon replied.

"Yon, you know that I also can send them back to the old school. I figured since you've been working so hard and have sent the triplets on their last few field trips, that I would give you a rest and send them back," Hither returned.

"That's very thoughtful of you, Hither. You're right, I am a bit tired," Yon said as he yawned and stretched. "I'd appreciate it if you'd take my place this time while I go find a soft cloud for a nap."

"Are you three ready?" Hither asked. They nodded. "Then hold hands and think back to exactly where each one of you was and what you were thinking when you slid down the slide and..."

Once again, as they thumped down into their school desks they saw what looked like white cotton candy swirling around them.

Chapter Eight

Jud Day

"It's sure good to be back," Jonathan said as he gave his old desk a hug.

"You three have been on quite an adventure!" Tique said with her usual caring smile.

"You're certainly doing what William Lowe had hoped when he built the old school with its powers and special features for field trips."

"You mean we're learning from the past, present, and future so we can grow up and use what we've learned to help others?" Nicholas asked.

"My, you have such good memories!" Tique replied. "So, what did each of you learn from all of this?"

As usual Jonathan was the first to speak.

"I learned that throughout history there has always been evil. No matter where we are, we have to be careful that evil does not grab us or take us in. But I also know there is much good in the world that we should encourage and support."

"A very worthwhile lesson Jonathan, especially

given your recent experience with a very evil Follower," replied Tique.

"And Nicholas, what did you learn?"

"I learned that the power of the old school we're trying to protect is probably some kind of magnetic energy combined with electricity and light. I found out that D.C Powers somehow helped William Lowe create this power for the school."

"Then your field trip was a success," Tique said. "And now you, Mikaia."

"I learned that we continue to be led by faith. This time the end turned out the way we'd hoped. I learned we have also been given more powers and will discover them as we need them. Eventually we will discover the power of the old school. Then we will be able to protect it and continue taking field trips to help others. At least I hope we do."

"You certainly have learned a lot. No wonder the Master Inventor is as pleased with you as I am. By the way, class dismissed!" exclaimed Tique.

The triplets ran out into the midday sun. Even though Nicholas and Mikaia had traveled through time twice and had gone to and from the antique shop, they had only used up about two hours of earth time.

"I say we go home and rest up a bit. Like Yon, I think I could use a nap," Jonathan said.

"That's not like you, Jonathan. You're usually the one ready to go anywhere," replied Nicholas.

"Well, you try getting snatched, tied up, thrown into the back of a bumpy wagon, dragged into a cave and left for spider bait, and then almost shoved down a shaft! See if that doesn't tire you out just a bit!" Jonathan answered.

"Actually, it makes me want to yawn just thinking about it. I say we head home and get some rest too," replied Nicholas.

"I'm with you on that," Mikaia added.

When the triplets got home, their mom was in the kitchen putting away some groceries and their dad was upstairs in his office, so they quietly climbed the stairs to their rooms to relax.

It wasn't long before the triplets all met in Mikaia's room, probably awakened by the smell of the pot roast their mom was cooking for dinner.

"You know, I laid in bed a long time just staring at this Timber Pine Mining Claim. Somehow I feel it means something. I wish we could figure out where this and the Creekside Mine were located. It has some kind of number description on it but I can't figure it out," Nicholas said still staring at the mining claim.

"Too bad we don't have the Creekside claim," Mikaia replied.

"What do you mean too bad we don't have the Creekside claim?" Jonathan returned.

"Didn't you tear it all up for the paper trail you left along the road?" asked Nicholas.

"And waste a perfectly good claim for my old

document collection? Of course not, I merely tore pieces off from around the sides of it. Ned took it from my pocket in the cave when he searched me. Since it was torn up, he threw it on the ground and stepped on it a few times. After he left, I picked it up and shoved it back in my pocket," Jonathan replied.

"Then you still have it!" Nicholas exclaimed.

"That's what I just said. I'll get it for you!" Jonathan ran to his room and soon returned with the claim.

"See, you can still read all the main stuff."

"This is great! Now we have a better chance of finding the Creekside Mine," Nicholas concluded.

"Maybe Dad knows what these numbers on the claims mean," Mikaia suggested.

"Yeah, he's a pretty smart guy," Jonathan added

"He may not be familiar with these numbers," Nicholas replied. "But it's sure worth a try."

"I think I hear Mom calling us to come for dinner," said Mikaia.

"Great! I'm so hungry I could eat a horse!" Jonathan replied.

"That's what I heard Mom was cooking tonight," said Nicholas

"No way! We don't eat horse, do we?" Jonathan asked.

"And you thought that was ground beef hamburgers we had last Saturday?" replied Nicholas.

"Well yes! You mean I ate a horse?" Jonathan

asked again.

"We do live in the country now, Jonathan," said Mikaia.

"Hey, Jonathan, bring the Creekside claim so we can show them both to Dad," Nicholas said.

"I ate a horse?" Jonathan said again in disbelief. "I thought that was just a saying!"

"Are you all washed up and ready for dinner?" asked their mom.

"You know Mom, I think I'll skip dinner tonight," Jonathan sputtered out. "I don't feel like horse again tonight."

"Does my beef pot roast smell that bad?" Cathy, his mom, asked.

"Beef, not horse?" replied Jonathan.

"Of course. We don't eat horse. I didn't even know you liked it. I guess I could try to find some if..."

"Oh no, Mom, not for me," Jonathan quickly replied. Both Nicholas and Mikaia couldn't keep from laughing any longer.

Jonathan looked over at them with a menacing look that only Jonathan could make. Nicholas decided he had better change the subject quickly.

"Dad?"

"Yes, Nicholas."

"Do you know much about land and location on deeds and claims?"

"A little bit. Why are you asking?

"We bought these two old mining claims and now

we're trying to figure out where they are."

"Pass them over, Nicholas, and let me take a look. Let's see, the Creekside and Timber Pine mining claims. I'm not sure exactly where these claims would be around here, but I do know what these numbers represent. It's a little complicated."

"What do they represent, Dad? We need to know." Jonathan stated.

"To find things in the world, the whole world has an imaginary grid of longitude and latitude lines drawn across it, from north to south and from east to west. These are numbered. Therefore, someone at sea, or in the sky or on the ground can know exactly where he is at any time.

"Our federal government used these lines to do a geological survey of the entire country so each state and the counties within the state would know their boundary lines. Then they divided these lines into what they call townships and ranges which are mile squares on the map. These mile squares were broken down into so many acres of land. By looking at the survey numbers, a farmer, miner or anyone would know exactly what property he owned and where it was. Someone who uses these numbers all the time would know how to read them."

"Who would know how to read them, Dad?" asked Mikaia.

"Probably someone working in real estate or mortgage banking, but for sure a surveyor. Surveyors use them all the time. That's what they do for a living, check property and land borders based on these lines. Did that help a little?" their dad asked.

"You were right. It was a bit confusing, but now I understand how people can find things. I also know we need to find a good surveyor to help us," Nicholas replied. "Thanks Dad!"

"Any time, Nicholas."

"How's the pot roast?" their mom asked.

"It's great, Mom, but I was kinda hoping for some horse," Jonathan said as he took a big mouthful and looked at Nicholas and Mikaia who smiled back.

"Well if you can find some I'll cook it up," their mom said still not really knowing what was going on between the triplets.

"Actually, I do prefer a slow cow to a fast horse," Jonathan found himself adding. Nicholas and Mikaia began to laugh again.

After dinner the triplets decided to meet in Mikaia's room. Nicholas stopped in the hallway for a moment before joining them upstairs.

"What were you looking for?" asked Mikaia as Nicholas held up the telephone book he'd just grabbed.

"I've got it," Jonathan said. "We're checking for land surveyors."

"And I have a suggestion," Mikaia added. "Let's first look up Jud Day!"

"Great idea! He's the man we met who was

surveying Pete Rider's property a couple of weeks ago," Nicholas added as he looked under "surveying" and found an advertisement for "Day Surveying Services."

"I'll grab the phone!" yelled Jonathan. He ran out and down the hall to Dad's office and brought it back.

"Thanks, Jonathan! Now let's see. Here's the number," Nicholas said as he dialed and listened. "I should have known that! He's closed for the day and the message said to call back between eight and five tomorrow."

"I'll write down the phone number and the address," Mikaia said as the phone rang.

"Should we answer it?" Jonathan asked.

"It's probably for Mom or Dad. Who do we know in Opportunity?" replied Nicholas as the phone rang a couple more times before their mom picked it up downstairs.

"Mikaia, it's for you," their mom called up.

Mikaia looked puzzled as she picked up the phone.

"Hello...who is this again? Oh, hi Ashlee. Now I remember meeting you...yes and Marie too. You're having a small party before school starts for a few friends and want to invite us?" Mikaia asked as she looked up at the boys.

"When is it? This Saturday afternoon? Just a second. Do you want to go to a party at Ashlee's? She thought that it might give us a chance to meet some of the other sixth graders from our school."

"Fine with me," replied Jonathan who was always ready for a party.

"It would be a good time to meet some of our class mates and make some friends...sure," Nicholas said.

"Sounds like fun, Ashlee. You say your address is 10034 County Road and the party's at four? Yeah, thanks for inviting us. See you in two days." Mikaia hung up the phone and said, "That was nice of her."

"This could be a lot of fun," said Jonathan.

"We all need to be careful what we say about what we've been doing this summer. We can't tell anyone about the old school's powers," Nicholas added.

"You're right. We can talk about fixing it up and playing there, but we have to be very careful," added Mikaia. "Agreed?"

"I'm in," said Jonathan.

"Me too," Nicholas added.

"Good!" said Mikaia. "Now, I'd better check to make sure Mom or Dad can drive us there and pick us up. It sounds a bit far to ride our bikes,"

"And I'll call Mr. Day's office first thing in the morning," Nicholas said.

"And I'm going to my computer and search to see what I can find out about these two old mining claims. Who knows, maybe Yahoo knows something we don't," Jonathan said.

"I'm pretty sure Yahoo knows a lot more than the whole town of Opportunity, Jonathan," Nicholas replied. "Good luck!"

A green Chevy pickup drove into the dark alley behind the Opportunity Grocery Store late in the evening. Before long a cream-colored Ford Taurus pulled up next to it and turned off its lights.

"The triplets are back, all three of them!" a stern high pitched female voice yelled.

"But I thought it was all set up to grab one of them and hide him back in 1858. Then they could no longer time travel. Cryptic even got a hold of my great grandfather, Ned, to do it," Phil Steward replied.

"Well, Ned messed up and everything fell apart when the other two were able to travel back in time again and find where he had hidden their brother," the high-pitched voice replied.

"How could two of them do that without the third? And how could they find someone hidden back it 1858? I thought that was impossible for them!" Phil stated.

"Apparently they've gained even more power to snoop around. Cryptic's very upset with us because we weren't able to do our part to stop them," the female voice continued.

"Well, Ned did snatch one, didn't he?" asked Phil.

"Yes, but when he found them trying to escape he went crazy and tried to kill them! That's not what Cryptic had told him to do. And because of that they got away!"

"What happened to Ned?"

"Let's just say it was a good thing for you that your father was born before this happened."

"You mean he was killed?" Phil shouted.

"I imagine a fall down a hundred-foot mine shaft would do it."

"Who did it? Was it the triplets? Cryptic?" Phil shouted back.

"Hey, keep it down! No, neither. He fell down the shaft when he tried to push all three of the triplets in. I imagine if he'd lived, Cryptic would have thrown him down the hole anyway. He doesn't like sloppy people who disobey him," the female voice explained.

There was silence.

"Anyway, Cryptic wants us to think of some other way to stop them and destroy their power. Weren't you a mining engineer before you retired?"

"Yes, in Mariposa County, after I moved from here."

"Cryptic feels there could be a link between the mines and the power William Lowe built into the old school to make time traveling possible from there. He wants you to look into it."

"I don't know...I'm not sure..."

"He's not asking you, he's ordering you!" the stern female voice responded.

"Years ago, I searched around and couldn't come up with any link between the mines and the old school," Phil whined back.

"Well you'd better try again, and harder. Cryptic knows of other mine shafts one could fall into around here!" the female voice could be heard saying over the sound of her car accelerating out of the parking lot.

Phil Steward sat motionless in his car for a moment wondering how he had gotten involved in all of this. Then his pickup's lights went on as he slowly pulled away.

Their mom had pancakes and bacon for breakfast. Jonathan was the first one down following the aroma of the bacon. Nicholas was close behind. Mikaia came down last again. It seemed to the boys that girls always took longer to get ready, so they didn't comment on it.

"What time is it, Mom?" asked Nicholas.

"I believe it's about eight-ten."

"Thanks," Nicholas replied as he made a bee line for the downstairs phone.

"Hello, is Mr. Day available?" Nicholas asked as he responded to the receptionist at the Day Surveying Services Office. "Oh, he's out on a job? When do you expect him back? Could I make an appointment with him, please? Great, ten-thirty would be fine. You're located in a small commercial building about two blocks north of the grocery store? Yes, thank you."

"What did he say?" Mikaia asked as Nicholas walked back into the kitchen.

"He was out but we have an appointment with

him at ten-thirty.

"Good job, Nicholas. Let's see if Mom is going into town this morning," suggested Mikaia.

"Do you have a meeting this morning?" asked their mom who was still working in the kitchen.

"Yes, we're going to meet with a surveyor, Mr. Day, to find out more about the mining claims. Are you going into town today?" Nicholas asked.

"Sorry, not today. We went in yesterday and I have a lot to do around here."

"Then we'll just take our bikes," replied Mikaia. "Do you remember the call I got yesterday, Mom?"

"Of course, I think it's the first one you've received."

"That was Ashlee Wilson, a girl we met in town a couple of days ago. She's having a before school party at her home for some of her friends on County Road tomorrow at four o'clock. She's invited all of us so we can meet other sixth graders from our school. Would you please give us a ride over and back?" Mikaia asked.

"I'd be glad to. It's about time you started meeting some kids your own age. You've spent most of the summer so far just doing things together. Sounds like a wonderful opportunity to make some new friends."

"That would be great!" replied Nicholas.

"Now don't forget your chores before you go into town this morning. You all remember what they are?"

"Of course, Mom. I'm washing all the bed linens,"

replied Mikaia.

"I'm planting out back the apple tree that Dad brought home yesterday," Nicholas added.

"And I'm knocking the spiders and their webs down, again, in the garage and barn. Any one care to switch?" asked Jonathan as Mikaia and Nicholas quickly disappeared.

Mikaia and Nicholas finished their chores by ten and ran out to the garage to get their bikes and meet Jonathan who was still knocking down spiders.

"Don't get bitten by one or you could become the next Spiderman!" Nicholas said, laughing.

"Matter of fact I've been bitten by two so far, a big black one and a small red one. I can't wait to see what I look like when I sneak into your bedroom tonight!" Jonathan replied.

"I'm not worried. If you were going to get sick or something it would have happened already," returned Nicholas.

"It took Spiderman a while didn't it?" Jonathan shot back.

Nicholas swallowed hard when he remembered what happened in the movie. "You don't have any swelling or jitters yet, do you?" he asked.

"No, I'm fine. I just can't seem to control my right arm," Jonathan said as he quickly swung his broom around towards Nicholas who ducked and jumped back with a surprised look on his face.

"Did I get some spiders on you? I could always

use a sidekick!" Jonathan added with a smile.

"Boys!" Mikaia shouted as she grabbed Jonathan's broom. "We have a meeting! And Jonathan, if your face swells up tonight, come to my room. I'd love to take some pictures of you! Now let's go!"

They all hopped onto their bikes and took the twenty-minute ride into town to the grocery store. After another two minutes down the road they found the small commercial building with one sign reading "Day's Surveying Services." They leaned their bikes up against the front wall and walked in.

"How may I help you?" asked a young lady in her early twenties with a flower tattoo on her left arm.

"We have an appointment with Mr. Day at ten-thirty," said Nicholas. "We're the Fraziers."

"I expected you to be a little older," she replied. She seemed to be confused by their young age.

"If you made an appointment, I'll check if Mr. Day can see you now," she said as she walked down the short hall.

"So, you're the Frazier appointment on my calendar," Mr. Day said as he emerged from his office. "You're a little young to want my surveying services, aren't you?"

"We actually need some help in locating two parcels of land," Nicholas exclaimed.

"Don't I know you three...You're the triplets I bumped into when I was surveying Pete Rider's land a couple of weeks ago, aren't you? Don't you live across the creek?"

"Yes, we do. I'm glad you remembered," returned Nicholas.

"Well come on in. Let's see if I can help you," said Mr. Day taking them down the hall and lining up three chairs in front of his desk.

"I'm Nicholas, and they're Mikaia and Jonathan."

"Nice to meet you, again. Now what is this all about?"

"Since we've just moved to Opportunity, we've become very interested in the history of the area. We recently purchased some old mining claims from the antique store and have been trying to figure out where the old mines were located," replied Nicholas as he handed Mr. Day the two claims.

"Let me see, the Creekside Mining Claim and the Timber Pine Claim. I've heard of those before from some early records and surveying I've done over the years. The geological survey location for the Creekside mine would put it right about here," he said as he stood up and pointed at a large map on his wall. All three triplets stood up and moved closer.

"And the Timber Pine Claim would be about here. Now that's really interesting that you'd purchase these two claims."

"Why is that?" asked Jonathan.

"The first one, the Creekside claim is right where your property is today! And the Timber Pine Claim is about a mile south-east of you right next to the property I surveyed earlier for Mr. Rider," he said looking puzzled.

"You mean that our property is the Creekside Claim?" Nicholas couldn't help shouting out.

"Pretty much," Mr. Day replied.

"Then that would put the Timber Pine Claim right where the old school property is located, wouldn't it?" asked Mikaia.

Mr. Day checked the numbers, then the wall map again. "Yes, right on the spot!"

"This sure is a coincidence," Mr. Day said as he sat back down. "I guess if you want to know about the Creekside Mine and the history of that piece of property you had better ask the person who owned the land before you, Harold Lowe," he said.

The triplets just stared at each other for a moment... then Jonathan spoke up.

"Why can't we find any traces of the old mine on our property or near the old school?"

"I can answer that. As the mines gave out the citizens here didn't want any dangerous tunnels around. So, they blew up the openings, leveled them, then spread out the mine tailings, you know the dirt the miners had brought out and piled up. Over time bushes and trees took over. That way the land looked better and more livable for the respectable folks who were moving in."

"So, the mine tunnels are still there, just covered

up?" Jonathan asked.

"Under these hills are miles of tunnels with a few still open. I sure hope this makes sense to you. Now you own the old mining claim for your own property. Go figure," Mr. Day added.

"Can you tell from the maps where the old mine openings are for these two claims?" Nicholas asked.

"From what I can see, and knowing each piece of property, it looks like the Creekside opening would be just about where your barn is standing today."

"And the Timber Pine?" Nicholas continued.

"Probably near or under the old school house, but I can't be sure of either unless I spend some time surveying," Mr. Day replied.

"You've been more than helpful, Mr. Day and we really appreciate your taking the time to answer our questions," Mikaia said as all three of the triplets stood up.

"Do you mind answering a question for me?" asked Mr. Day.

"Oh, no, not at all," Nicholas replied

"How come you ended up buying the very claim that your property sits on?"

All three looked at each other and hoped that someone would have an answer. Finally, Mikaia spoke up. "Mr. Day, do you believe in dumb luck?" she asked.

"Yes, I suppose I do," he returned.

"Then for three sixth graders to bump into

something like this, I would say it has to be just dumb luck! Don't you agree?" asked Mikaia.

"Now that you put it that way I can't really disagree... Well, hope to see you again sometime." Mr. Day walked them out with a very perplexed look on his face.

"Good job Mikaia," Nicholas said. "I wasn't sure what to say to him."

"I can't believe it. No wonder the area looked familiar to us back in 1885. There are probably tunnels under our barn and under the old school!" Jonathan said as he scratched his head.

"I don't think this is really dumb luck," Nicholas said as they slowly pushed their bikes back up the street towards the grocery store.

"I don't either, but I had to say something," replied Mikaia.

"Matter of fact, I feel like this summer has been a long string of clues left for us by Harold Lowe, alias, Halo," said Nicholas.

"It seems as soon as we get one thing figured out, we get two more to solve," Jonathan exclaimed.

"Halo did ask us if everything always seemed to work out the way we hoped, didn't he?" asked Jonathan.

"Yeah, that's when he told us we had to have faith in the Master Inventor and the powers He's given us...I guess," replied Nicholas.

"Besides, he said that he was always watching us,"

Jonathan said.

"I hope he had his eye on us back in the mine when Ned almost killed us," replied Mikaia.

"You know, maybe he did. We did swirl out of there just in time and even ended up back in Midst instead of the old school. Things do sort of work out, but they can get really scary too," added Nicholas.

Chapter Nine

The Tunnel

"Do you think we should stop at the hardware store and buy an extra shovel?" Jonathan asked.

"A shovel?" questioned Mikaia.

"We're going to do a lot of digging in the barn looking for the tunnel. aren't we?" Jonathan asked.

"I guess an extra shovel so both you and Nicholas can dig would be useful," said Mikaia.

"What do you mean, me and Nicholas?" replied Jonathan.

"You don't expect me to dig, do you?"

"Of course! Just because you're a girl," Jonathan said loudly, "doesn't mean..."

"I'm going to buy a tool also!" Mikaia yelled out.

"Then what are you going to buy?" Nicholas asked.

"An auger!" Mikaia quickly replied.

"A what?" asked Jonathan.

"It's a tool used for boring holes, in this case a long-handled tool that drills deep into the ground," Nicholas said as Mikaia nodded and smiled back. "It's something like a post hole shovel."

"And what's that?" Jonathan replied.

"It's like an auger," Nicholas said as he shook his head.

"So what good is a small hole you can't climb down?" Jonathan replied.

"I'll be testing the ground for hollow or soft spots, looking for the tunnel or softer dirt used to fill the opening in. When I find some, you and Nicholas can start digging there. It could save us a lot of time."

"Great idea, Mikaia!" said Nicholas. "That way we don't dig up the whole barn!"

Jonathan looked at Mikaia and asked, "How did you know about an auer, or agar, or..."

"An auger!" Mikaia replied. "Because I read about it in a book on ranching that I got in the library when I heard we were moving out here."

"You read about it?" Jonathan replied.

"Yeah, in a book. You ought to try it sometime," said Mikaia as she pushed her bike ahead of the boys. Jonathan looked at Nicholas and shrugged.

"How did you know what that was?" Jonathan asked Nicholas.

"I read the same book," Nicholas said as he pushed his bike up next to Mikaia.

"But I've been reading some very important historical documents!" Jonathan cried.

When they entered the hardware store, they didn't see Evelyn Hawkins at her usual spot behind the counter. They walked over to the gardening supplies section and picked up a sharp trenching shovel and a long-handled yard auger.

"This is what an auger looks like. You hold it like this and push down and twist it around," Nicholas demonstrated.

"Boy, Mikaia, you're going to have a lot of fun making all those holes with this heavy thing," Jonathan said smiling. Mikaia frowned when she tried to pick it up.

Just then Sam Hawkins came in from the back storage room.

"Thought I heard someone come in, Oh, the Frazier triplets," he sputtered, "all three of them!"

"Why not all three?" Mikaia quickly asked.

"Urr, I'd heard that one of you was gone visiting a relative, yeah, a cousin or someone," he replied.

"Nope, we're all here and doing fine," said Mikaia walking towards the counter with Jonathan and Nicholas who were carrying the shovel and auger.

"We missed seeing your grandson, Arnold, and his friend, North, out at the old school. They said they planned to play there a lot, but we haven't seen them all day," Mikaia decided to add. She couldn't help smile a bit.

Sam just looked at her for a moment not sure what to say. "Yeah I heard that too. I guess they found something they liked to do better."

"How much will these be?" Nicholas asked.

"Fifteen dollars for the shovel and twenty-five for

the auger," Sam replied as he stared at all three of them.

"Didn't our dad open a charge account with you the other day when he was working on our air conditioning unit?" asked Nicholas.

"Yep, he sure did!"

"Then we'd like to put this on the Frazier account, please," Nicholas stated.

"I guess that would be all right. Here's your receipt for $43.10," he said as he handed Nicholas a copy of the slip he'd signed.

"Thanks for your help Mr. Hawkins. Look forward to seeing you soon," Jonathan replied.

Outside by their bikes Jonathan said, " Mikaia, you sure know how to push Mr. Hawkins' button."

"I just had to do it for all the trouble he and the other Followers have caused us. Besides, going into his shop knowing he and Evelyn are Followers, always gives me the creeps. I felt that a chance to keep him on his toes would make me feel a bit more comfortable."

"At least you entertained me," Nicholas said as he patted Mikaia on the back.

"How are you guys going to carry the tools back on your bikes?" Mikaia asked.

"How come us?" asked Jonathan.

"That's okay, Jonathan. We'll each just lay one across our handle bars and pump back up the hill a little harder. As you know, Mikaia needs to save all her strength for the auger," said Nicholas and he and Jonathan began to laugh.

When they got home they found both of their parents in the kitchen just starting a grilled cheese sandwich lunch.

"You made it back from town just in time," Cathy, their mother said.

"If you hadn't, I might have eaten all the sandwiches," their dad, Nathan, added.

"What do you have there?" he asked when he saw the tools they'd brought in to show him.

"We hope you don't mind but we charged these on your account at the hardware store. We'll pay you back," said Nicholas.

"That's fine with me as long as you have a good reason for buying them," he returned.

Nicholas took a few minutes and explained to his mom and dad about meeting with Mr. Day and showing him the mining claims. He told them, that Mr. Day felt that the Creekside Mine opening was probably under their barn and that the Timber Pine Mine was under the old school.

"I can't believe it! That's sure is a coincidence," their dad said.

"That's what Mr. Day said," replied Nicholas. Then he explained how most of the mines had been sealed and the tailings spread out so they could make the area look better.

"Then what are the shovel and the auger for?"

their dad asked.

"We thought we'd try to find the entrance to the Creekside mine so we'd know where it was and which direction the tunnel went."

"I guess that's not a bad idea, son. That way we could be aware of any potential cave- ins or drainage problems when we're working the property. Just be careful and don't dig up the entire place. Be sure you cover your holes back up so none of us step into them."

"We will, Dad," Nicholas said as he took a bite of a sandwich. He tried to catch up with Jonathan before the stack of sandwiches in front of them was gone.

After they had finished lunch, they hurried out to the barn.

"Anyone have any suggestions?" Nicholas asked.

"Why don't we look around for dirt that looks different or spots that seem to have sunk," suggested Mikaia.

"Good idea!" said Nicholas as they all headed off in different directions.

"You know, there have been thousands of boots walking all through this barn over the last hundred years and a lot of this dirt probably has been moved around," Jonathan noted.

"I say Mikaia starts using the auger right about now," Jonathan said with a smile.

"You're not going to hold me to that are you? That

thing is heavy," she said.

"That's the tool you wanted us to buy for you, isn't it?" asked Jonathan smiling.

"All right then, I'll try it right here," Mikaia said as she pushed the auger down in the very center of the barn and began turning and lifting the dirt out of the three-inch-wide hole she was making.

After about fifteen minutes of digging, Mikaia's arms were so weak she could barely lift the auger. Jonathan came over and took it from her. He heard a faint "thank you" as she collapsed onto a nearby hay bale.

All together they made six holes about five feet deep around the barn.

"The first five holes each took almost twenty minutes to drill, this one only took ten," Jonathan said. "That means it must be softer dirt, maybe even fill dirt. I say we start on this hole."

Nicholas brought over the new trenching shovel, stepped on it, and tossed out the first shovelful to his right. Jonathan grabbed the older rounded shovel as they both began to dig.

After a long time of digging and tossing another shovelful of dirt to the top of the hole now even with his head, Jonathan said, "I don't think this is the spot. It's all the same kind of dirt and it's getting even harder to dig."

Meantime Nicholas had been making a few auger holes around the sides of the barn.

"Hey, look at this dirt," he yelled out as Jonathan and Mikaia came over. "It has some small rocks mixed in with it and some of them look like quartz."

"It looks a lot like the dirt we saw those two men bringing out of the Creekside Mine when we met D.C. Powers," Mikaia said as she took a closer look.

"That's it!" said Jonathan.

"How'd you know that?" asked Nicholas.

"When you get thrown on it and have to sit in it for a long time, you know what it looks like," Jonathan replied.

"I guess you did get kind of close up and personal with mining dirt around Opportunity," Nicholas said.

"Matter of fact, I believe I still have some in my pocket from when Ned threw me down," Jonathan said. He reached in his pocket and pulled out a few rocks and some dirt. "Look at this. It's the same as that dirt!"

"You're right, this could be the spot," Nicholas said.

"I can't believe you're wearing the same clothes you had on yesterday when you were snatched and tossed in the dirt!" Mikaia said.

"I like to help out a little around here and not make Mom wash my clothes too often," Jonathan returned. "It saves water!"

"Well, I think it's about time you started worrying about air pollution!" Mikaia said as she held her nose and stepped back.

"Get the shovels and we'll try here," Nicholas stated.

Jonathan grabbed both the trenching and the round nosed shovels and they started to dig.

Mikaia picked up an old square-nosed shovel and began filling in the deep hole Jonathan and Nicholas had dug earlier, happy to be away from Jonathan who was smelling rather ripe.

"When's that party tomorrow at Ashlee's?" asked Jonathan.

"I think Mikaia said it was at four," Nicholas replied.

"I'm looking forward to it. I haven't been to a party for some time, besides Ashlee and Marie are kind of cute. If that's any indication, then their other girlfriends could be cute too," Jonathan said with a big smile.

"That would be fine with me. I'm hoping to meet some people our age who can be our friends and who aren't kids of Followers," Nicholas returned as he threw out another shovelful of dirt.

"Yeah, it would be good to relax once in a while," Jonathan said, tossing out the next shovelful.

The boys dug for almost an hour and saw the same mixture of quartz and dirt to a depth of almost six feet.

"Good thing you pushed that seven-foot ladder into the hole or we'd never get out," said Jonathan.

"And I'm thinking we'll probably hit water before

we find the mine opening or its tunnel," Nicholas said.

"That's quite a hole you've dug. Have you had any luck?" they heard their dad say.

"Wow, you surprised me!" said Jonathan. "I was in this digging trance just bopping along."

"No, but we do know this is probably some of the fill dirt. There's just so much of it!" replied Nicholas.

"Why don't you three take a break? We have a special visitor I know you'd like to meet."

"Who is it, Dad?" Nicholas asked as he climbed up the ladder.

"Now that part is a surprise," their dad said as they all headed towards the house.

As they approached the house, the triplets passed by a blue BMW with Florida plates parked in front of their garage.

When they walked in the front room, they spotted a tall man in his late thirties talking with their mother. He had brown hair and deep blue eyes and looked vaguely familiar.

"Mikaia, Nicholas, and Jonathan," Dad said, "I'd like you to meet Henry Lowe, the son of the man who sold us this ranch.

They all stood there for a moment remembering when Harold Lowe had told them how disappointed he was that his son wasn't going to stay in Opportunity and be the custodian of the old school, a job they had now.

After a moment Nicholas spoke up. "Sorry, Mr. Lowe, you just caught us by surprise. It's nice to meet someone who enjoyed this ranch as much as we do."

"I'm glad to hear that and glad to meet all of you," he replied as he shook each of their hands.

"Henry was just telling us that he has driven to California because he has several meetings in different cities over the next ten days. He thought he'd drop in and see his old home," their mother explained.

"You're welcome to look around all you want, Henry," Dad said.

"I'm actually considering moving back to the area. My father wanted us to settle around here, so I thought I might give it a shot. When he told me he'd sold the house, it was quite a letdown. I hadn't had a chance to tell him what we were considering," Henry explained.

"How is Harold doing?" asked Dad.

"He seems to be busier than ever, in and out all the time. He bought a small house just down the street from us in Orlando and often helps with our six-year-old son and eight-year-old daughter. He's a wonderful granddad."

"I'm glad to hear he's adjusting so well to retirement," their dad replied.

"You know, if you don't mind I would like to look around a bit. I haven't been to the old ranch for many years."

"We'd be happy to show Mr. Lowe around, Dad," said Mikaia.

"I'd like that!" said Henry.

"Great idea," Dad replied. "Have a good tour."

Mr. Lowe and the triplets walked out to the front of the house where he just stood for a moment looking around.

"Mr. Lowe?" Mikaia asked.

"Just call me Henry," he returned with a smile.

"Did you ever take field trips when you were young?" Mikaia asked.

Nicholas and Jonathan were caught off guard for a moment by her forward question.

Henry paused for a moment before he looked down at her. "Yes, Mikaia, I did, several times."

"Then you know about the Master Inventor and the old school?" she continued.

"Probably almost as much as you do," he returned looking at the triplets to see their expressions.

"Then you know about us and our powers?" she asked.

"My father has great trust in me and has kept me informed of some of the things that you three have accomplished and I am very impressed," Henry said as he slowly started walking towards the barn.

"My father had high hopes that I would take over as the custodian of the old school just like he had done for my grandfather. But even with the knowledge and trips I'd been on, I became bullheaded and decided I didn't want to do it. It was a lot of responsibility and I'd always wanted to leave the ranch and be on my own. So, I went away to college, received my mechanical engineering degree, married and tried not to think about the power and chance to help others I'd selfishly given up. I even moved to Orlando, Florida, to be as far away as I could from Opportunity. Just recently I've been rethinking my decision."

The triplets looked at each other wondering what this would mean to them if Henry came back as the old school custodian.

"Things seem to have gotten more complicated since we arrived," Nicholas said.

"In what way?" asked Henry.

"It's turned out that there are more Followers of Cryptic than anyone had imagined and they're doing their best to try and stop us from taking field trips and protecting the powers of the old school," Nicholas replied.

"That's what I have heard. It's quite a difficult job for the three of you especially since you are so young. But I've heard you've managed to outsmart and even stop Cryptic's evil Followers in their tracks, frustrating Cryptic to no end."

"We have been very lucky, but we know we're being helped along by Halo and the Master Inventor," Nicholas said.

"It's really strange having a father who turned out

to be a guide for the Master Inventor. At first it was hard for me to understand. Later on, it just felt normal until I began to feel the job of custodian wasn't for me. I'm not sure if it was the uncertainty of the field trips or the awesome responsibility of the knowledge I gained and my ability to use it to help others. Now I feel I might have been wrong to give it up."

"Do you know where the powers of the old school come from?" Jonathan chimed in as his brother and sister looked over at him, not sure if this was the appropriate time to bring that up.

Henry looked at Jonathan for a moment.

"Actually, Jonathan, I didn't have your powers to travel where I wanted or a curious mind that was strong enough to figure out that I needed to find its source to protect it,"

Henry replied. "From what my father said I do know there is some kind of relationship between the ranch and the old school and its power."

As they walked into the barn, Henry stood there for a moment looking at the deep hole the triplets had just dug under the loft near the back wall.

"Looking for gold or just going tunneling?" Henry asked.

"We're trying to find the filled in opening to an old mine that was on the property in the 1800's," answered Nicholas.

"Well, good luck. I know there were mines all over

these hills. Who knows what you'll find, maybe even the secret of the old school's power," he said as he winked.

"Do you really think you might want to come back as the custodian?" Jonathan asked.

"I'm not sure. I do have a good job and a family in Florida, but if I decide to return you'll be the first to know."

"I think I hear Dad coming," said Mikaia," so we better be careful what we say."

"I understand," replied Henry.

"How's the tour going, Henry?" their dad asked.

"The triplets are excellent tour guides and we've had a chance to talk and share some old stories about the place. Now I think I should be going. I have to be in Sacramento by tonight. I really enjoyed meeting all of you and seeing the ranch again. It gives me a lot more to think about," Henry said. He walked out of the barn and towards his car with the rest following him.

"Come back anytime, Henry. It's good to see you. Next time plan on staying for the night and bring your family if you'd like," their dad said as Henry started to pull away.

When he turned and waved he said, "I'd like that. Thanks again."

"It was interesting to meet Henry, but now I've got to get back up to my office and put in a few more hours. See you later," Dad said, heading over to the house.

"Thanks, Mikaia for getting us alone with him for a few minutes. I wasn't sure what to make of him," said Nicholas.

"We did find out what we needed to know. He did go on field trips and his father, Halo, trusts him enough to fill him in on some of the things that are going on," Jonathan added.

"Apparently Halo still feels that Henry would make a good custodian for the old school," Mikaia mentioned.

"Where would that leave us?" asked Jonathan.

"I'm not sure, but I'm certainly not going to worry about it until it comes up again. Right now, I want to do some more digging. Henry felt there was a relationship between the ranch and the old school too," Nicholas added as he walked back toward the barn.

The triplets dug their hole deeper and Nicholas even started another one next to it.

"We keep bringing up the same kind of dirt. I know we must be near the opening but I think we'll need a large backhoe to get down deep enough to find it," Nicholas said.

After another three hours of digging Nicholas climbed out of the second hole and sat down on a hay bale.

"Well Mikaia is certainly right," Jonathan said.

"I am?" asked Mikaia.

"I'm so sweaty and dirty now that I'm sure I'm polluting the air. I need to take a shower for sure," he said and climbed out of the first hole and flopped down on the ground.

"This doesn't seem to be getting us anywhere. Maybe we should go and look around the old school. Maybe we can find where the opening was for the Timber Pine Mine," Mikaia suggested choosing a broken hay bale to fall onto since it was softer. "Or maybe we should forget about tunnels for a while."

"Was there someone else in the hole with you, Jonathan?" asked Nicholas as he moved towards the hole Jonathan had just climbed out of.

"It's big enough now to hold our school's basketball team, but I was alone down there. Why'd you ask?"

"I thought I heard a voice coming from down there," Nicholas replied as he looked in.

"I didn't hear anything. I think you've been working too hard," Jonathan replied, approaching the hole.

"Be quiet and listen," Nicholas said as he got down on his knees next to the hole and cocked his head to listen. "Maybe I hear wind from a tunnel or we found an underground river, but I keep hearing something that sounds like a soft 'ooop'."

"I can't hear anything," Jonathan said, putting his head way down in the hole.

"I think I hear it!" Mikaia said. She had worked

her way over and was now kneeling down over the deep hole. "Yes, I'm sure I hear it. It does sound like a soft and airy 'ooop', whatever that means."

"I guess I've got too much dirt in my ears," said Jonathan. "Do you think it's Halo speaking to us through the wind or something again?"

"I'm not sure, but I'm still hearing it," Nicholas said.

"You know, coming from down there it could be Cryptic speaking. I always figured that he probably lived somewhere down deep in the earth," Jonathan shared.

"You've been seeing too many of those scary movies I keep warning you about, Jonathan!"

"It's probably Halo trying to help us along. He said he liked to use the wind," said Mikaia.

"Shush, I hear it again," Nicholas said. "It almost sounds like 'up'."

"What does that mean?" said Jonathan. "The mine tunnel is down if it's anywhere.

The voice should be saying 'downnn' not 'oop'!"

"Well there is an up, you know," Mikaia said.

"An up?" asked Jonathan.

"Yes, an up," Nicholas said as he stood and looked up at the loft above them.

"The loft? Why there's only hay and a view from up there," replied Jonathan.

Nicholas jumped up and grabbed the old rope that lowered the ladder down.

"Okay, I'll help you pull it down and go up too if it means taking a longer break from this digging," Jonathan said as he helped Nicholas with the rope.

When the ladder swung down, all three of them climbed up to the hay loft. Jonathan pulled the loft doors open and looked out.

"Yep, same fine view," he said.

Nicholas walked along the side of the loft that was over the hole they had been digging. He stopped a couple of times and rapped his knuckles against the boards.

"What are you doing, checking for termites?" Jonathan asked with a laugh.

"I know what he's doing," Mikaia said as she began tapping on some boards next to Nicholas.

"Do you see it, Mikaia?" he asked.

"Yeah, it looks like this side of the barn is built out further from the wall than on the other side of the loft.

Jonathan's curiosity kicked in and he moved over to take a look. Then he also started tapping on some boards.

"It sounds kind of hollow, but right here it sounds solid," he said.

"These boards above me are cut across and aren't solid all the way up," Nicholas said standing on his toes.

"And these four at the bottom aren't nailed tight to the loft floor," Mikaia returned as she knelt down below him.

"Maybe they're loose or something," said Jonathan. He walked over and gave the lower boards a swift, hard kick.

"Hey, take it easy..." Nicholas started to say as the lower boards swung in towards the wall and the top boards swung out into the loft.

"That's like a spinning door of some kind!" Jonathan said.

"Look, there's a dark shaft between this wall and the outer barn wall that drops down!" Mikaia exclaimed as she looked in. "And it looks like there's a ladder nailed into the wall!"

"Man, this is great! I wonder where that goes." Jonathan said as Nicholas climbed down off the loft.

"Where are you going at a time like this!" yelled Jonathan.

"Flashlights!" Nicholas yelled back, running out the barn door towards the house.

"Good idea," shouted Jonathan.

Jonathan and Mikaia could see that the four six-foot boards were bracketed onto a horizontal bar, which was also attached through brackets on the inside. These allowed it to spin open if it was hit hard. The opening it made below was about three feet high and four feet wide, plenty of room for someone to climb through.

"Here's a flashlight for each of you," Nicholas said as he climbed back up.

"I'll go first," Jonathan volunteered. "I'm getting used to dark tunnels," he added as he slowly descended down the ladder followed by Nicholas then Mikaia.

"Let's try to space ourselves so there's not too much weight on this thing at one time. The wood is really old and some could be rotten," Jonathan advised as they moved themselves further apart.

"Man! This thing goes down forever. We left earth about thirty feet ago. Hey! There's the bottom," they could hear Jonathan say as they saw his flashlight flashing around below.

"It's damp but not bad," he yelled up.

Once on the bottom they all slowly followed the tunnel as it sloped even further down.

"Boy, I'd give five dollars to know what direction we're going," Jonathan said.

"We're going slightly south-east," Nicholas replied. "Can I have my money now?"

"How do you know that?" Jonathan asked. Nicholas pointed his flashlight at the compass he'd brought along. "You sure do think of everything, Nicholas. Okay, I owe you three dollars and fifty cents."

"What happened to the five you said you'd pay?" asked Nicholas.

"Remember that ice cream I sprung for when we were in town and you didn't have any money?"

"Yeah, you said it was on you!" Nicholas replied

as they dropped further into the cave.

"Yes, but I also said I'd keep track...so I'm keeping track," Jonathan returned.

"Okay, three fifty then," Nicholas said, shaking his head.

"Done!" replied Jonathan.

"Don't you two think we should keep quiet and listen, just in case?" asked Mikaia.

"Good idea," Nicholas said, "now that I've got my three-fifty."

Chapter Ten

The Cavern

"Hey, a tunnel splits off to the left and right, which way should we go?" Jonathan asked.

"Keep following the main tunnel as long as it goes slightly south east," Nicholas replied as he checked his compass again.

"Be careful not to trip on these ore car tracks," said Jonathan.

"Where did those come from?" Mikaia asked.

"They just started along the main tunnel after the other tunnels cut in," said Jonathan. "Boy are they rusty!"

"The air sure smells in here. It's so still and stale," Mikaia said.

"It's probably because we're following Jonathan," Nicholas replied.

"Usually I'd argue with you, but I think you're right, whew!" agreed Jonathan. "And with all the tunnels sealed this air could be one hundred years old! No wonder they died young in those days. It wasn't the tough life. It was the stinky air!"

"Another tunnel goes off to the right! Do we keep

Mikaia found herself holding onto the side of
the tunnel

going straight, Nicholas?" Jonathan asked.

"You've got it."

"I'm getting a little claustrophobic in this place," Mikaia said quietly.

"It's getting wetter. The ceiling is dripping!" Jonathan said.

"If my calculations are right, we're probably going under our creek right about now, I hope," replied Nicholas.

"Should I expect to see the roots from apple trees next?" Jonathan asked.

"If you're lucky and the roots are this deep, 'Yes.' I'm betting the Creekside and Timber Pine Mine are directly connected," Nicholas replied.

The tunnel started moving slowly back up, and then turned up sharply. Mikaia found herself holding onto the side of the tunnel to help pull herself up.

"Help me!" the boys heard Mikaia scream from behind them. They both turned around but didn't see her.

"Mikaia! Where are you?" yelled Nicholas.

"Did she fall into a shaft?" Jonathan asked, hurrying back.

"I don't think so. We would have seen it!" Nicholas yelled as he started running back down the tunnel. "I don't see her flashlight anymore, either."

"She couldn't just disappear, could she?" Jonathan said. "Hey, quiet! I think I hear her."

Nicholas worked his way back up the tunnel. They

both stood still for moment and listened.

"Did you hear that, Nicholas?"

"Yeah, it was Mikaia yelling, 'Help, I'm in here!' But where's here?"

"I hear it faintly again. It's coming from this side of the tunnel, but there's nothing there," said Nicholas.

"Wait a minute. I've got an idea," Jonathan said as he pushed his flashlight up against the tunnel wall a few times. All of a sudden, the flashlight disappeared.

"What was that?" Nicholas asked.

"It's like an invisible curtain of some sort! I can put my flashlight and arm against the tunnel wall and they go through."

"Try your leg," suggested Nicholas.

Jonathan kicked his leg out towards the spot where his light had disappeared.

"Your leg went in too," Nicholas said. "I'm ready. Let's see if our whole body can get through. We've got to find Mikaia!"

He jumped towards the side of the tunnel and found himself in a gigantic cavern that had a dim white glow. Mikaia was standing there looking around in amazement. They both turned as Jonathan jumped in.

"What the..." Jonathan got out before his mouth dropped open.

"Mikaia, are you all right?" Nicholas finally asked.

"Yeah, I reached out for the tunnel wall to pull myself up and fell right through!"

"What is this place?" asked Jonathan.

"What is this invisible wall stuff, anyway?" Mikaia asked.

"I think we might have found the source of power for the old school!" Nicholas replied.

"How do you figure?" asked Jonathan.

"Why else would somebody put up an invisible tunnel wall? Besides who are the only people we know who could have done such a thing?" replied Nicholas.

"Good point," Mikaia responded as she started walking further into the cavern.

"This sure took some time to dig. It's got to be at least sixty feet high and eighty feet wide, and I'm not sure how long. It seems to keep going," Nicholas said as he followed Mikaia.

"Nicholas, touch the side of the cave," Jonathan suggested, standing to the right against the wall. "Most of it looks like quartz with a few rocks and dirt mixed in like the stuff we were digging up, and some strange copper wiring woven around each quartz piece."

"Yeah, but this cave is mostly quartz rock. It's all glowing and making the dim white light we see," replied Nicholas.

"Look a-ways in front of us," Mikaia said. "There's a big mound of dirt right in the middle. I wonder why they left that."

"Maybe they didn't have time to take it out," suggested Jonathan.

"Look about fifty feet behind it," Nicholas said. "Another tunnel comes in."

"Let's check it out!" Jonathan exclaimed as he turned his flashlight back on and strode into the tunnel with Nicholas and Mikaia right behind him.

"Which way is it going, Nicholas?" asked Jonathan.

"Slightly north-east," Nicholas replied as the new tunnel began to slope up.

"Do you think the power of the old school is up this tunnel?" Jonathan asked.

"Actually, we should be close to the old school by now," Nicholas replied.

"We'd better be! We just ran out of tunnel," said Jonathan as he pushed up against the dirt to see if it had an invisibility curtain too. "Darn, now we have to go back."

"No, we don't," Mikaia said. "Shine your light straight up."

"Hey, a shaft! It was so dark I didn't even see it. I think I see a ladder hanging down inside," Jonathan said, "but it's too high up for me to reach."

"What if I get on your shoulders, Jonathan, and see if I can reach it?" suggested Nicholas.

"What if Mikaia gets on my shoulders instead. She's lighter and I may need my back for the trip out!"

replied Jonathan.

"Okay, Nicholas, boost me up!" Mikaia said.

She stepped into Nicholas's hands and climbed up onto Jonathan's shoulders as he held his hands up over his head to support her.

"Now balance and hang on!" Nicholas said as he moved around into position.

"I've got a hold and I'm going to put most of my weight on the ladder and pull at...watch out!" Mikaia yelled. The extension ladder quickly slid down and hit the tunnel floor with a loud thump as Mikaia grabbed Jonathan around his head.

"Climb down, Mikaia! You're pulling my ears off!" Jonathan exclaimed. "Next time you can be the tree, Nicholas."

"Nicholas?" Jonathan questioned when he saw him disappear up the ladder.

"We found it!" Nicholas yelled back down.

"What?" replied Mikaia.

"The old school, I'm standing in it right now! Climb on up and take a look!"

"Unbelievable," Jonathan said as he climbed out through a low cabinet door and out into the old school with Mikaia right behind him.

"Why this is the very cabinet we reached into when we pulled out Ronnie and Donnie's lunch pails a few weeks ago," Mikaia noted.

"And the back is a hidden entrance to the tunnel! Go figure!" added Nicholas.

"So, there was a tunnel between the Creekside and the Timber Pine Mines!" Jonathan said. "I guess it was a good thing Mr. Powers had a claim on both of them."

"That's fine, but we still don't know the source of the power for the old school," Nicholas pointed out. "Let's back track through the tunnel on our way to our barn and see if we missed anything. We need to head home soon anyway. We are on earth time. It's getting close to dinner and Dad will come looking for us."

"I agree. We can't just disappear from the barn. If Dad doesn't see us we'll have some fast talking to do," Mikaia said as she crawled back through the low cabinet door."

"We're right behind you," replied Jonathan.

"I still can't figure out this large cavern," Nicholas said as they re-entered the glowing cave.

"And this huge mound of dirt in the center, what gives with it!" Jonathan said as he kicked at it. "Hey! My foot went through! I think it's another invisibility curtain!"

They all felt the mound of dirt and found that their hands went through.

"That foot of yours really comes in handy, Jonathan," Mikaia said.

"Let's see if we can go inside," suggested Jonathan as he jumped forward.

Making a loud thumping noise, he fell back out holding his nose. "Man, that smarts! I hit something hard just inside."

"I'll go in, slowly," Mikaia said.

She pushed her flashlight in front of her. "This must be it!" she yelled as she disappeared.

The boys cautiously followed her in.

Covered by the large invisibility curtain, camouflaged to look like dirt, was a large machine of some sort. It was covered with rust but the parts that needed to move seemed well lubricated and in good shape. In the middle were six gigantic magnets, three on each side of a large space, wrapped with miles of copper wiring.

"This looks like the electrical transfer station we have just outside of Opportunity," Nicholas said, "There are Generators, capacitors, transformers, all kinds of stuff surrounding those large magnets! I recognize them from the field trip our class took to the power transfer station near us in San Francisco."

"This has got to be it!" said Jonathan as he reached out to touch one of the many wires that led down into the ground.

"I wouldn't touch that if I were you!" Nicholas shouted. "We don't know if that's a live wire or not. You could get electrocuted."

"Thanks! Good point," replied Jonathan as he quickly put his hands into his pockets.

Meanwhile, Mikaia had walked back through the curtain and was looking intensely around the large cavern. The dim light from the cavern walls was beginning to flicker.

"You know what this looks like to me?" she said as her brothers pushed through the curtain and saw the flickering light. "This cave is some kind of large generator that uses magnetic and electrical power. The cave must provide the light and electricity that are somehow bent and spun to allow a slipping of time which makes time travel possible."

"From what we've learned so far, you've got to be right, Mikaia!" Nicholas said.

"But how does it do it? How does it know when we slide down the slide, or spin on the merry-go-round that we need to get to Midst?" Jonathan asked.

"I don't know, but somehow it does," replied Mikaia.

"Maybe that's where the Master Inventor's power enters it," Nicholas added as they looked around.

"We need to get back soon," Mikaia finally said.

"You're right. Let's go," Jonathan added.

"Right about here is where we came in," Nicholas said as he moved his hand along the cavern wall until it pushed through. "This invisibility curtain is something. We could walk right by and never know this place was here."

"That's probably the idea," Jonathan replied as they stepped out into the cave and turned to their right towards home.

"Shuush!" whispered Mikaia. "I hear voices coming from down the tunnel!"

"You what? Wow, I hear them too! Who in the world would...?" Nicholas started to say.

"Quick, let's move back into the cavern," Jonathan said as they stepped back through the curtain.

The curtain stopped most of the sound from coming through, but the triplets could hear voices in the tunnel just on the other side of the curtain.

"I don't know why you had to drag me along, Phil," an angry female voice was saying.

"Well I told you, even as a mining engineer, it's hard for me to find my way around through all these mine tunnels. Besides, you didn't believe me when I told you I'd been all through these tunnels before and found no evidence of any power source for the old school!"

"Yeah, and I was with him the last time we looked too," said a familiar voice.

"Hey, that sounds like Sam Hawkins!" Mikaia whispered, "and the other one must be Phil Steward."

"I think you're right," Nicholas replied quietly. "How'd they find this place?"

"And just up here we'll hit the end of the tunnel and have to retrace our steps. I figure we're under the school property now. Do you see any power source?" the triplets heard Phil Steward ask.

"Of course I don't, but it has to be somewhere. It can't be in the trees!" the high pitched angry voice replied. "And I do expect you to keep looking until

157

you find it! We have to destroy this power or we risk being destroyed by Cryptic!"

"Let's wait for a moment," Mikaia suggested, "until they hit the end and turn around and head back. We'll follow them and see how they got in."

A few moments later the triplets could hear them going back.

"I told you so. It sounds like what one of those Frazier kids would say, Phil!" the high-pitched voice smirked as they passed.

The triplets stepped out and followed them using only one flashlight that they carefully pointed down at their feet. Just after they'd gone under the creek they heard the voices get softer.

"Look, they turned off to the left and went up this tunnel," Jonathan noted from the voices.

"That tunnel leads towards the Hole-In-the Mountain Mine. If that's where it ends up, then there has to be some kind of entrance Phil Steward found near it," Nicholas said, looking at his compass. "We'll need to check it out later."

"We'd better hurry!" advised Mikaia.

They walked as fast as they could through the tunnel. When they got to the ladder that led down from the barn loft, they could hear their dad calling their names.

"Quick, let's get up onto the loft," Nicholas said. They hurried up and through the swinging door and onto the loft.

"Mikaia, Jonathan, Nicholas, where are you? It's time for dinner!" their dad called from the front of the barn. "You didn't dig to China, did you?" he said with a chuckle.

"No, Dad, we're all up in the loft!" Mikaia yelled down.

"You three got so worn out you decided to nap?"

"Something like that, Dad," Nicholas yelled back.

"Well come on in and wash up, Mom's got some great horse burgers on the barbecue!" said Dad.

"I told Mom I didn't really want any horse meat!" Jonathan yelled back quickly.

"Just kidding, Jonathan." His Dad laughed and headed up to the house.

"Man, I'm never going to live that one down!" replied Jonathan as Nicholas and Mikaia smiled.

They climbed down from the loft and ran up to the house.

After dinner they all met in Mikaia's room again.

"Who was that lady we heard today?" asked Jonathan.

"I'm not sure. It doesn't sound like anyone I know," Mikaia replied.

"It wasn't Phil's wife, Mabel, was it?" Nicholas said.

"From what I remember of Mabel Steward I don't think she'd be capable of traipsing around in old mining tunnels," Jonathan replied. "And it sure didn't sound like Sam's wife, Evelyn, from the hardware store."

"Then how about Miss Ivy, after all she did want to buy the Timber Pine Mining Claim before we did," Nicholas suggested.

"You could be right," replied Mikaia. "We need to watch out for all of them now that we know they've found the tunnel. They could stumble through the curtain just like I did!"

"At least now we know what we need to protect," Jonathan added. "I'm not sure how we're going to do that. We can't stop them from going into the mine...unless we find the opening they used and fill it in!"

"Good idea, Jonathan. That would slow them down a bit, but Phil would just have another tunnel dug. He is a mining engineer you remember," replied Nicholas.

"Besides, if we do that they'll know that someone is trying to hide something from them in the tunnels and look even harder," Mikaia returned.

"Watching the old school is one thing. Keeping an eye on a maze of underground tunnels is another!" Nicholas added.

"I say we take another field trip tomorrow!" Jonathan suggested.

"And where would you want to go?" asked Mikaia.

"I don't care! Remember, I do have adventure in my heart!"

"We know, Jonathan. You're always ready to

move out and do something new which I enjoy too, but sometimes you have to make sure everything is okay right where you are," replied Nicholas, "like filling in some deep holes in our barn."

"Darn, we have to talk to Halo about that. If he's going to guide us using the wind, I wish he'd do it before we do all kinds of work!" Jonathan complained.

"We don't have to do it all tomorrow. We need to save some energy for Ashlee's party," Nicholas suggested.

"That's right, at four. Now that may be an adventure!" Jonathan exclaimed.

Chapter Eleven

The Party

In the morning the triplets got up early and hurried out to the barn. They each picked up a shovel and started filling in the holes they'd dug the day before.

"I'd prefer almost anything to this," Jonathan said as he pushed the last pile of dirt into the first hole.

"How about strange, dark mines with your hands and legs tied?" Nicholas asked as he tossed the first shovelful of dirt into the second hole.

"True, that does come in first, but this is a close second!"

With a break for lunch and some bacon, lettuce, and tomato sandwiches, they had finished by two o'clock.

"Looks like new to me!" Mikaia said. "Good job!"

"It sure is," Dad said when he came in to check on their progress. "I thought it would take you all day! By the way, I'll be the one dropping you off at the party today. I have some business in town to take care of. We'll leave about three-fifty, if that's all right."

"That would be perfect," returned Mikaia as she quickly headed out the door.

"Why are you in such a hurry?" Jonathan yelled, leaning his shovel up against the wall.

Running up to the house, she yelled back, "Because we only have two showers for three people, that's why!"

"Darn! That's right!" Jonathan exclaimed as Nicholas slipped past him just behind Mikaia.

"Darn, again!" Jonathan yelled.

He started walking slowly up towards the house shouting at Mikaia and Nicholas, "You'd better save me some hot water or you'll all be sorry...everyone at the party who can breathe will be sorry!"

Jonathan waited until the last minute to take his shower to be sure there was enough hot water. In their new school clothes, the triplets descended to the kitchen.

"This should be fun for you, a chance to finally meet some classmates," their mom said. "What time do you think Dad should pick you up?"

"We're not sure how long the party is going to last," Mikaia replied.

"Then why don't you take my cell phone and give us a call when you're ready," Mom suggested as she handed Mikaia her cell phone.

"Good idea, Mom," Mikaia said, "but I don't think it will be too late."

"Are you all ready?" their dad asked.

"Let's go! It's 10034 County Road, the Wilson place," Jonathan said as they headed down their road to the main highway.

Ashlee's home was a large single-story ranch style house about two miles north of town, with a half circle drive-through driveway. On one side were grape vines and on the other was an orchard of apple trees.

"Thanks, Dad. We'll call when it's over," said Mikaia.

She closed the car door and all three strode up the walkway. Jonathan knocked on the front door and within a minute Ashlee opened it.

"Hi, I'm glad you could come! This is my mother, Peggy Wilson. She's keeping the food table full for us."

"Nice to meet you Mrs. Wilson," Mikaia said. "I'm Mikaia Frazier and these are my brothers, Nicholas and Jonathan."

"Nice to meet you," Nicholas said and Jonathan nodded.

"And it's nice to meet the three of you too. I've heard a little about you already from friends who were at the school board meeting a few weeks ago. You three have been very busy this summer cleaning up the old school and everything," she said smiling. "Please come in."

"Follow me. I want to introduce you to some of my friends and classmates," Ashlee said, taking

Mikaia by the arm.

They went through the family room where a big table was set up with bowls of chips, potato salad, barbecued chicken, cookies and pizza. The triplets could see a bunch of kids in the patio by the swimming pool. Some of them had brought their suits and were swimming.

"Oh, hi!" Marie said as she hurried over. "I'm sure glad you came! I wanted to get to know you better too!"

She quickly pushed them back towards the house as they heard a loud splash and a light spray of water hit them.

"That's just Chuck. He loves to do cannon balls off the board, but he makes a very large splash," Marie said as the triplets looked over and saw a boy so large he could barely pull himself up out of the pool.

"We'll keep an eye out for him," said Nicholas.

"Hey, you two should try out for the football team," a voice said as an athletic-looking boy came up.

"I'm Calvin Hill. I moved from Oakland three years ago to get away from the entire ruckus there and I love Opportunity! You'd make a great lineman," he said to Jonathan. "And I can see you as a wide receiver," he added looking at Nicholas.

"Are you the team Captain or the team recruiter?" Jonathan asked.

"Actually, a little bit of both. I'm the Captain of

the Offense and Brad Owens here is the Captain of the Defense."

"Hi guys! Good to meet you!" Brad said. "Where did you move in from?"

"We were raised in San Francisco," Nicholas replied.

"Great city. But I've been a country boy all my life, you know, hanging around horses, cows, and an occasional chicken when my dog grabs one," he said as they all laughed.

"By the way, Ashlee, has that fresh pizza arrived yet?" Brad asked.

"Yes, I saw my mom put it on the table a moment ago," Ashlee replied.

"You can't beat Wong's Pizza. You've got to try some! Follow us over!" Brad said as he and Calvin headed towards the table.

"I want to introduce them around some more first, Calvin," Ashlee said and pulled them towards a group sitting around a patio table eating pizza and chicken.

"All of you, I'd like to introduce Mikaia, Nicholas, and Jonathan. They just moved into Opportunity at the start of summer from San Francisco."

"Most of the kids in the group said 'hi' or nodded as they kept on eating.

Ashlee continued, "These are my friends, Tamara, Shana, Larry, Will, Shelby and Justin!"

"Nice to meet all of you," Mikaia replied.

"If you want to know where all the hangout spots are around here, you can ask me or Ashlee," Larry said. "We'll be glad to show you around."

"And I'll help too!" Marie added walking over from the pool.

"We'd like that," Jonathan said glancing at Marie and noticing her dark brown eyes twinkling in the sunlight.

Then Nicholas saw Jonathan's smile change to a frown. When Nicholas turned around, he saw Arnold and North walking towards them.

"Oh, Arnold, North, I'd like to introduce you to..."

"We've meet them already Ashlee," Arnold said.

"Nice to see you again," Mikaia found herself saying unconvincingly, as Arnold nodded to her and North just stood still.

"What have you two been up to since we saw you last?" Jonathan asked stepping a little closer to Arnold.

"I've just been doing some summer chores at home for my Granddad. I always like helping my Granddad. He has me doing interesting things, like hanging around during the day at the old school," Arnold said with a smirk. "Matter of fact I'm working on something for him right now."

"So, you decided to hang out at the old school again. I'm glad to hear you're not wasting your time. That can be awful boring after a while," Jonathan replied.

"I hope you're successful at finding a place to fit in here in Opportunity," Arnold said.

"Well, if I'm really lucky, I may even be in the same class as you. I'd like that," said a smiling Jonathan.

A loud thud came from the pool as a large wave of water crashed down over Arnold and North.

"Chuck! You're going to pay for this!" a soaking wet Arnold yelled.

Nicholas, Mikaia, Jonathan, Ashlee and Marie couldn't help but laugh.

"Arnold can be annoying at times, but he's mostly just talk. Now North, none of us have figured him out yet. He won't do anything without Arnold," Ashlee said as she and Marie took the boys by their arms and led them over to the table where Peggy Wilson had just unboxed the fresh pizza.

"I hope you like pepperoni and sausage," Ashlee said.

"That's our favorite," Mikaia replied as she and her brothers each took a piece.

"I like the music selection you're playing, Ashlee," Nicholas said. "You have a great variety of types and styles."

"Those are some of my favorites. I've hooked my iPod up to our speakers. Do you really like it, Nicholas?" Ashlee asked.

"Yeah, I do."

"My mom said it would be okay if we danced at

the party," Ashlee replied.

"Danced?" said Nicholas, obviously caught off guard.

"Sure, you just put your arm around me and then we move to the music."

"Yeah, I do know what dancing is, but I...I...just wore these old tennis shoes that won't move well on this carpet," Nicholas managed to get out.

"We could go outside on the patio. They'll probably work better on that surface," Ashlee suggested.

"Maybe, after I get my fill of this delicious pizza," said Nicholas quickly grabbing two more pieces.

"Then do you like our little town after being raised in a big city?" Marie asked as she looked at Mikaia and Jonathan.

"Yes, very much! We love exploring the history of the town and the people. There is so much to discover and learn about the gold rush and mining and everything," Mikaia said.

"We really like all the mining tunnels you have all over the place," said Jonathan realizing he may have said too much.

"The mining tunnels, I thought they were all covered up?" Marie replied.

As Mikaia gave him a sharp poke with her elbow Jonathan said, "I mean we saw some old mine claims and maps at the antique store. They are very interesting."

"Oh, the old maps. Yes, there is a lot of history in these foothills," said Marie smiling. Her brown eyes continued to sparkle as she looked at Jonathan who had decided he needed to be holding two pieces of pizza.

The triplets had a good time meeting many of the students from Lowe Middle School and they received various invitations. Mikaia was asked to join the girls' soccer team and to try out for cheer leading.

Calvin encouraged Nicholas to start practicing with the football team. He was also offered a backup spot on the Academic Team when some of the kids found out he'd been selected for it in San Francisco.

Brad Owens tried to persuade Jonathan to try out for a defensive line position on the football team and then the following season the wrestling team. Both boys did 'dance around' to avoid Ashlee and Marie's continued hints about the great music.

Around eight o'clock they noticed that the party was winding down so Mikaia called their dad to pick them up.

"We've really enjoyed ourselves and it was nice of you to give us a chance to meet everyone," Mikaia said when Ashlee and Marie walked them to the door.

"It was great," Jonathan said as Marie gave him a big smile.

"I really liked all your friends, Ashlee," said Nicholas, "and the music and food."

"Maybe next time I'll have a dance party," Ashlee

replied. "Would you come to that?"

"Ah...sure, if I wasn't in the middle of football or something," Nicholas answered.

"Then I'll check with you first," she said.

Nicholas swallowed hard and smiled.

Outside the door they found Arnold and North waiting for them.

"Just wanted to let you know about that interesting thing I'm doing again for my Granddad," said Arnold.

"You mean hanging around the old school, again?" Mikaia asked.

"Yeah, and we just happened to be there yesterday afternoon about five looking in the old school house window, and guess what we saw inside?"

The triplets froze for a moment realizing what the answer would probably be.

"I don't know, bats?" asked Mikaia finally.

"No, the three of you, just standing inside. Funny thing is we'd been outside most of the day and didn't see you go in. When I told my Granddad he was very interested. He gave North and me both twenty dollars and told us to keep up the good work. Just thought you'd like to know that. Hope you had a good time at the party," he said chuckling and walking back into the house just as the triplets' dad drove up.

"Darn! Now we know they'll go back into the tunnels to find out how we got in and probably search inside the school too," Jonathan said.

"You're right. Let's meet in my room when we get home," said Mikaia waving at her dad.

"How was it? Make any new friends?" he asked.

"There was no trouble making friends, Dad. They all seemed very friendly and wanted us to do and join all kind of things," Mikaia replied.

"Some were very friendly, weren't they Nicholas?" Jonathan said.

"I do like Ashlee, but man the girls around here are aggressive. Before I had my first piece of pizza she wanted to dance...and no one else was dancing!" Nicholas replied as the rest of them laughed.

"Well you had the same problem as me, Jonathan, except you and Marie kept eyeing each other."

"Yeah, I thought I'd have to be dancing soon too," Jonathan replied.

"This won't help much, but it gets worse," their dad advised. "By your junior or senior year in high school you boys will be doing most of the asking. What you don't know is that the girls will still be manipulating things to get what they want. That goes on forever, but it can be fun as long as you realize it."

"It sounds like we don't have a chance," Jonathan replied.

"That pretty well summarizes it, Jonathan," their dad said with a laugh.

"Not all girls are like that," Mikaia said.

"Okay, name one girl you know that isn't," Nicholas challenged.

"Well there's ... and... well I'm not like that!" Mikaia exclaimed.

"At least not yet," Jonathan added.

When they arrived at home, the triplets thanked their dad and headed up to Mikaia's room.

"How are we going to handle this?" Jonathan asked.

"I don't know. We can't continually keep guard over the old school much less spend all our time in the tunnels," Nicholas replied.

"We could put some well-placed thin fishing line throughout the tunnel and in the old school. At least we'll know that if it's disrupted, they've been there," Nicholas suggested.

"Not a bad idea," Mikaia said. "It certainly wouldn't hurt anything and might let us know when and where they're sneaking around."

"Then let's do it first thing in the morning," Jonathan said. "Besides I want to follow that tunnel Phil and Sam came through and see exactly where it comes out."

"Yeah and I bet it's one of the two old mines just south of us," Nicholas said.

"I'll put new batteries in our flashlights and get the fishing line and a knife to cut it," Jonathan added.

"Good idea! I'm game," Mikaia said.

"And I'll pull a few old nails out of that old barn

wood out back," Nicholas replied.

"Why do we need old nails?" Mikaia asked.

"Something to secure the fishing line to. There aren't many places to tie it in a cave. Besides, if they happen to find one of the old nails, they'll just think the miners dropped it when they were putting up the wooden beam supports," Nicholas replied.

"You're always thinking, aren't you?" Jonathan returned.

"As much as I can, but I don't have all the good ideas in this group," he added.

The next morning the triplets walked to the barn and climbed down into the mine tunnel from the hidden space in the loft. They made their way to the place where another tunnel crossed and the ore car tracks started. Jonathan placed fishing line trip cords across the tunnel in both directions, securing them with two nails that he stuck in the ground about two inches off the tunnel floor. A little ways up, just before they went under the creek, another tunnel turned off to the right.

"This is the tunnel Phil took yesterday. Let's follow it and see where it comes out," Nicholas said. They all turned right and walked as fast as the dark tunnel allowed.

About ten minutes later the tunnel started going up. A couple hundred feet later the tunnel was partially filled with dirt and narrowed so much that they could barely slip through.

"This must be where they filled this mine in," Mikaia said.

"Look, I see some light!" Jonathan replied. He pushed two loose boards aside and squeezed through.

"This is it. We're out," Nicholas said as they looked back at the narrow mine entrance that cut into the mountainside. "This has got to be the Hole-In-the-Mountain Mine."

"You're probably right from what I remember when we hiked up the road passing this turnoff to the Tunnel Mine," Mikaia said.

"We can hardly see the opening. Someone had to work a bit to open it up enough to get through," Nicholas said.

"And this is where they came in," Jonathan added pointing down at fresh footprints next to several different tire tracks.

"I think I hear a car coming up the dirt road," Mikaia yelled. "Quick! Back into the cave! It's too open to hide out here!"

Quickly they all squeezed through the opening. Nicholas went in last so he could see who was driving up. Through the green Chevy pickup truck window, Nicholas made out Phil Steward in the driver's seat but couldn't see his passenger.

"It's Phil again with someone I didn't have time to see. Let's hurry down the tunnel and get into the cavern behind the invisibility curtain," he said and they all started moving down the tunnel.

Chapter Twelve

Powers Discovered

At the junction the triplets turned right passing under the creek and climbed up the steep tunnel to the cavern entrance. They could hear voices getting closer behind them. Quickly, they all felt along the wall until they found the narrow space hidden by the curtain and then jumped in.

"I sure hope they don't find this place," Mikaia said quietly, hearing them just outside the curtain.

"This tunnel ends just a hundred feet further. It's got to go somewhere!" they heard Phil say. "Sam said his grandson, Arnold, saw the triplets in the school, but he hadn't seen them go in, so one of these has to lead us there."

"You're the mining engineer, you figure it out!" said a high pitched female voice.

"The lady's back again too," Nicholas whispered as the voices went by.

"Yeah, thanks to Arnold's spying!" Jonathan whispered back.

"You don't hear someone coming from the tunnel behind the machine, do you?" Mikaia asked.

"Something is making noise back there. We'd better hide!" Nicholas whispered. "Quick, let's get under the invisibility curtain covering the machine."

"Well, I'll be! I can't believe I found this place after all these years," they heard Sam Hawkins say. "This has got to be something important. It leads right up to the cabinet in the old school! I wonder where it goes out at?" he mumbled as they heard him walk by.

"That dim light sure helps a lot. I'll just look for any kind of footprints and follow them. The people who dug this had to get out too," he continued.

The triplets all swallowed hard and tried to soften their breathing so they wouldn't give themselves away.

After a few minutes they heard Sam's faint voice. "These prints all lead right up to the side of the cave...and...I can hear Phil's voice through the wall...or...impossible! Hey, Phil over here, follow my voice. There's some kind of invisible curtain here! Come on in! It's got to hide the school's power or why the magic?"

"Quick! Here's our chance now that they're at the far end of the cavern. Let's make a run for the old school and get out or we'll be trapped," Mikaia whispered. They snuck out through the old school side of the curtain and made their way into the back tunnel.

"Hold on for a moment. We can always beat them up and out of the school. I want to hear what they say and see if they find the time machine," Nicholas said as they stopped about twenty feet into the dark tunnel.

"This has got to be it!" shrieked the female voice. "It's just what I expected except its empty! Maybe that shining quartz with the wires attached that are all over the cave is the power source...maybe that's the machine!"

"No wonder I couldn't find this place! An invisible shield...even a mining engineer wouldn't know to look for that. I wonder how William Lowe did it?" muttered Phil Steward.

"Why is there a big pile of dirt over there?" asked Sam.

"It's probably just some diggings miners didn't want to take the time to get out if they didn't need to. In those days they were in a hurry. If they didn't have to move it, they left it!" Phil said.

"Do you think the quartz and wires could be the machine?" the lady asked.

"I know mines—not electricity and exotic time machines—but it looks to me that the size of this cave and the thousands of quartz crystals wired together could be the machine," Phil replied.

"Well I say we blow the whole thing!" said Sam, "and be done with it!"

"Yes, I agree. Cryptic would be very pleased with us. The sooner the better!" the high voice said.

"Then I'll get some dynamite from my hardware storage room and be back this afternoon to take care of the job!" Sam said.

"Just bring enough to shatter the quartz walls. I don't want any loud noises or obvious cave-ins or explosions. It could draw attention and damage the old school. If that happens there'll be plenty of questions asked. With our tire tracks and all of us driving up here yesterday and today, the authorities could trace things back to us." the high voice said.

"Okay then, just enough to shatter this place! It will be my pleasure!" Sam replied.

"Let's get out of here!" said Nicholas. They turned and went up the last thirty feet to the ladder that was already pulled down.

They climbed up the ladder and crawled out through the cabinet and carefully made their way to the front window and peeked out.

"Do you see anyone?" Mikaia asked.

"Just Sam's pickup truck!" said Jonathan.

"Let's look out the window on each side, just in case Arnold and North are hanging around," Nicholas suggested.

They each crawled over to a different window and looked out.

"Nope, looks clear to me," Mikaia said.

"Then let's climb out the back window and sneak

around to the orchard again, to be sure we're not spotted," Nicholas said.

"Let's do it!" Jonathan agreed.

They slid out the window and headed for the orchard.

"Look!" Jonathan said, "Just in time. Here comes Sam! I guess the other two are going back through the tunnel to Phil's pickup."

"We've got a field trip to take, pronto!" Nicholas said.

"To find Halo, right?" asked Jonathan.

"Right!" Mikaia agreed.

"As soon as Sam leaves, run to the slide! That's the quickest way to get to Midst. We just slide down," Nicholas said.

When Sam's truck disappeared, the triplets ran over to the slide. Jonathan went up the ladder first, taking his usual spot, followed by Mikaia, then Nicholas.

"All right," Mikaia said, "on ready, set, go, push off and think Midst!"

They slid down the slide floating into the swirling cotton candy and landed on the clouds of Midst.

"We made it! Thanks to a quick trip down the slide," said Jonathan letting out his breath.

"Of course you did, but you really didn't need the slide," said Yon.

"Yon, they're here for some help. They need to talk to Halo right away," Hither said.

"What's this about the slide?" Mikaia asked.

"It's just Yon mumbling again," Hither said.

"I don't mumble. I may murmur or grumble off and on and sometimes hum, but not mumble," Yon shot back.

"Okay, so you don't mumble. It was probably a grumble, then," Hither said.

"I told you it wasn't a mumble," Yon said as he smiled.

"Yon, we have to call Halo for them!"

"Well why didn't you just say so?" Yon asked.

"I'll call him, then," Hither said as he shook his head.

Suddenly they heard a popping noise. "Thought you'd be looking for me," declared Halo.

"Are we glad to see you!" said a relieved Jonathan. "Some of the Followers have discovered the cavern where the time machine is located. Sam Hawkins is going back to his hardware store to get enough dynamite to shatter all the quartz and wiring. He hopes this will destroy the machine's power source and maybe even the machine if he finds it!"

"Yes, I'm aware of this," Halo said. "You were very clever to discover it."

"Do you know everything that is happening?" asked Jonathan.

"Mainly just the things I feel I need to know, Jonathan, not everything."

"What can we do to stop him?" Mikaia asked.

"First of all, if they haven't found the machine and only blow up the interior walls of the cavern without them falling in, they won't destroy the power. The quartz is just a light source. The power actually comes from deep in the earth through wires that transmit intense electrical magnetic energy. You would still be able to go on field trips using the slide, the swings, and the merry-go-round. If the cave crumbled in on the machine, then the playground's power to take you on field trips would cease."

"Then you would no longer need us as custodians," Mikaia said.

"On the contrary, the Master Inventor wants you to keep growing and learning. He is very pleased with the three of you. He knows with your caring souls and other positive personality traits you'll help many people."

"But our power to time travel would be gone! How could we do it?" Nicholas asked.

"As Yon slipped up and told you, you don't need the power of the old school anymore. You can use it if you like, but like I said earlier, the Master Inventor increased your powers and gave you some almost as great as mine."

"What are these powers?" Jonathan asked.

"It is now time for you to know. Remember when you were in Sunday school a few years ago and you learned a little story using your hands to make a church and the steeple?"

"Yes, I do," Mikaia said. "We'd weave our fingers together bent down into our palms and point our thumbs up. Then we'd say as we held our hands up, 'Here's the church,' and then we'd point our index fingers up and say, 'and here's the steeple.' Then, as we pulled our thumbs apart and turned our hands up and wiggled our fingers, we'd say, 'Open the doors and see all the people.'"

"Very good Mikaia," Halo said and smiled.

"I remember that," Jonathan said.

"Well, you don't use the rhyme but you do weave your fingers together the same way and point your index fingers up, like you did with the steeple. Then you simply think of when and where in time you wish to travel, and why you need or desire to travel there. Then you'll hear a popping noise, just like I make when I travel, and you'll be there."

"Won't we use Midst or Hither and Yon anymore?" Nicholas asked.

"Yes, but only when you need to travel fifty years or more into the past or future. Then they will still need to send you."

"Wow! This is amazing, Halo," Jonathan exclaimed.

"You still should all travel together. Together your powers are increased. However, you can travel individually if it's necessary. Just use the time slide sign you make with your hands."

"The Master Inventor trusts us with a very

powerful tool," Mikaia said.

"He's watched you three and knows you won't abuse your power or His trust."

"It's not going to make Cryptic very happy that we can slide through time like he can," said Nicholas.

"That's true, but now his Followers really can't hurt you. They can disrupt you or hurt others around you yes, but not hurt the three of you. Cryptic himself would have to intercede to harm you using every source of power he has. However, to help you, the Master Inventor has given you one more power."

"Some other power?" Jonathan asked.

"Yes. Have you heard people say that they have intuition or insight? Or know something before it happens? Or were super sensitive to things happening around them?"

"My friend back in San Francisco said she had intuition," said Mikaia.

"Well, the three of you do have it now. You can think of it as intuition or insight."

"How does it work?" Jonathan asked.

"This is something you're going to have to learn and develop on your own. You'll each find it helpful to you in different ways. Again, it's a gift to be used to allow you to help others. You'll find it when you need it."

"There is so much to understand, Halo. What about the cavern and Sam Hawkins?" asked Nicholas.

"By now you should see that it won't make much

difference what the Followers do to the old school. You'll still have all its powers and more. You'll still be the custodians of the old school, but you won't have to get your power from it."

"Halo, did you know that your son Henry came to visit us and told us he may move his family back to Opportunity?" Mikaia asked.

"Yes, I've seen him change his mind on the importance of a lot of things lately. Now he knows that family, friends, community, and love are much more important than a powerful job and money. He's trying to change and I'm encouraging him to. If he does move back to Opportunity, he will be a strong ally of the Master Inventor. He knows how to take field trips but will only be able to do so if the old school's power is still strong and if he continues to have a caring soul."

"So, he'd be able to help us?" Nicholas asked.

"Actually, if he comes back he'd be able to support you, for you three are the custodians!"

"We may not be the custodians of anything if Sam and Phil and that lady have their way," Jonathan stated.

"Did you see who the lady was?" asked Halo.

"No, we just heard her angry voice. She doesn't seem like a very nice person," Nicholas said.

"It would help if you could find out who she is. That way you can watch out for her," Halo said.

"But what about the cavern?" Mikaia asked.

"How you handle this is up to you...you are the custodians."

Just as Halo smiled at them they heard a popping sound and he was gone.

"Darn, I wish he'd help us more!" exclaimed Jonathan.

"He has always helped us," Nicholas said.

"You're right, but sometimes I wish he'd help a little more," Jonathan replied. "What do you think we should do now?"

"We need to get back home and figure this thing out," Mikaia said.

"Yeah, let's get back and think things over," Nicholas replied.

"Hither, Yon, would one of you send us back to the old school?" Mikaia asked.

"Weren't you listening?" Hither asked. "We'd be glad to, but you can do that yourselves. You can actually send yourselves right home if you want."

"We don't have to go to the old school and see Tique anymore?" Jonathan asked.

"No, only if you go on a random learning field trip or travel more than fifty years to the past or ahead to the future when one of us sends you," Yon replied.

"So, all we have to do is weave our fingers into our palms and put our index fingers together?" Jonathan replied.

"Just use the time slide sign and think of where and when in time you wish to travel and why you need to travel there," Hither answered.

"Then I think I'll try it," Jonathan said. "Halo did say we could travel alone, didn't he?"

"If it was necessary," Mikaia said.

"Well I think it's necessary to try it out and see how well it works so we'll know," Jonathan replied. "We'll meet in Mikaia's room."

"He's right about each of us trying it out," Nicholas said. "I'll be right behind you."

"Then I'll follow you!" Mikaia said. "And Jonathan, if you get to my room first don't touch any of my stuff, okay?"

"You've got it," said Jonathan as he closed his eyes and thought hard with his fingers pointing up. With a loud 'pop' he was gone.

"I hope he was thinking hard. I'd hate to have to find him in a cave somewhere again," said Nicholas, who also made the hand-slide sign, then popped, and disappeared.

Jonathan found himself standing in the middle of Mikaia's bedroom.

"Man, this is unbelievable!" he said. He noticed her bedroom door was open and quickly closed it.

Nicholas almost bumped into Jonathan, but Jonathan jumped back upon hearing the popping noise next to him.

"Hey, be careful," Jonathan said.

"I'm working on it," Nicholas replied. "This is amazing," he continued, as he wiggled with excitement.

Both boys stood back from the middle of the room when they heard Mikaia's popping noise. She appeared with an expression of disbelief on her face.

"It's like taking a picture. You see where you want to go and 'pop' you're there!" she said. "What a way to travel!"

"You know, we're going to have to be very careful when we use this power. When Cryptic finds out what power we have, he'll look for ways to make us use it for selfish or evil purposes. He'd love to get us on his side through trickery," Nicholas said.

"That's another reason for us to try to travel together, so we won't be tempted to do something silly," added Mikaia.

"You're both right. We should agree as to what we're going to do and how we're going to do it. That way we can always watch each other's backs and know what to expect," Jonathan said as Mikaia and Nicholas nodded.

"So, what are we going to do about Sam Hawkins?" asked Jonathan.

"We know that he doesn't destroy the old school or the playground because three weeks ago we stopped him from burning it down a year from now in the future. So, we either stop him today from blowing up the cavern and possibly hurting the old school and the playground or he doesn't try," Nicholas said.

"Knowing Sam, he is going to try. Either we have to hope he doesn't find the machine and hurt the old school, or we have to do something to stop him," Mikaia replied.

"I say we stop him. Why should we let him blow any of it up? We are the custodians, aren't we?" said Jonathan sounding a little too confident.

"We are, but we still need to be careful," Mikaia replied.

"Sam's going to have to bring a lot of dynamite if he wants to shatter the inside of that large cavern," said Nicholas as he stood thinking.

"So?" Mikaia shrugged. "Keep going."

"Moving a lot of dynamite is illegal without the proper permits."

"But Sam owns the hardware store. He probably has a permit to ship it," Jonathan said.

"I'm not sure. He probably has it shipped, and then he sells it in smaller quantities. Besides, I don't think he's allowed to store it in town anyway. It's too dangerous. If he is keeping dynamite in his hardware store room like we heard him say, then it's probably there illegally," said Nicholas.

"Bingo!" Jonathan said. "Then I'm sure the police would want to know about all that dynamite being stored in town. At least the other shop owners would like to know about it!"

"You're right," Mikaia said. "We should notify the Sheriff. If they find him at his store loading up his truck full of dynamite, he'll have to do some real fast talking!"

"Then that's our plan. We'll have to move fast and time this just right if the Sheriff is going to catch him at his store," Nicholas said.

"He's probably there by now," Jonathan said. "I could go and watch him and let you know when he starts loading."

"Good idea. How far do you figure the police department is from his store?" Nicholas asked.

"If they left right away, about three minutes," Mikaia said.

"Then I'll go with you, Jonathan, while Mikaia goes to the police station. As soon as you and I see Sam loading up, I'll pop over to the trees behind the police station and go in and let Mikaia know. By the way, Mikaia, why don't you ask for the Deputy named Stan, the friend of Mrs. Roddy? He sounds like he moves fast when he hears there's a problem," Nicholas suggested.

"Good idea, Nicholas. Let's do it!" Jonathan exclaimed.

"Okay, Nicholas, let's think about being right behind the hardware store by the trash dumpsters so we can stop this guy!" Jonathan said.

"I'm with you," Nicholas said.

They both made the hand-slide sign and closed their eyes. Mikaia did the same and heard two pops just before she disappeared.

Jonathan and Nicholas reappeared behind a dumpster about fifty feet away from the back of the store.

"Look, Nicholas, there's his truck, backed up to the storage room door. He's bringing a box out...and now he's bringing out another. Looks like dynamite to me."

"I'd better be on my way. He looks like he's got plenty," Nicholas said as Jonathan heard a pop.

As Nicholas entered the Sheriff's Office he saw Mikaia walk over to the desk officer and ask if Deputy Stan was available. The deputy looked at her for a moment then picked up his phone. In less than a minute a man with wavy brown hair appeared.

"I understand you asked for me?" he said looking at Mikaia.

"Yes, I heard you mentioned around town as someone people could count on."

"Well, I'd like to think they can," he said as he smiled.

"My brother and I are worried about the friends we have in town who work in the shops."

"Worried?" he said, "in what way?"

"Is it legal to have a lot of dynamite stored in town?"

"Dynamite, of course not. Why are you concerned about dynamite?"

"We're afraid it might go off and hurt our friends."

"And where is this dynamite?"

"A man in a pickup truck, that's backed up to the hardware storage room, is loading boxes of it right now," Mikaia said, trying to add a little quiver to her voice.

"How do you know this?" Deputy Stan asked in a much more serious tone.

"My brother just told me." Mikaia said as she pointed to Nicholas who was still standing by the door. "We were sure you'd want to know and felt it was the right thing to do...you know, to tell you," she added.

"You're certainly right, young lady. What is your name?"

"I'm Mikaia Frazier."

"Well, Mikaia, we'll just have a quick run over there and check on this." Stan said as he walked towards the back offices.

Within a moment Deputy Stan and another deputy appeared.

"Now you wait here for a while if you please," Deputy Stan requested. They quickly left as Mikaia nodded.

Meanwhile, Nicholas had worked his way to the back of the police station and popped over to where he had left Jonathan.

"Wow! You scared me! I guess I've got to get used to that. Are the police on the way?" asked Jonathan. Nicholas nodded just as a green Chevy pickup appeared.

"Looks like he's got some help," Nicholas said, "and it looks like Phil Steward!"

"Are we in luck, two for one!" Jonathan whispered.

"Glad you finally got here. I'm going to need help getting this dynamite through the old school cabinet and into that cavern," said Sam.

"And you're sure this is a good idea, Sam?"

"Of course it is. How else are we going to stop them unless we destroy their power source?"

"Well what about all this dynamite. What if I drop it?" Phil asked nervously.

"Don't be such a whiner! You'd have to jump on it before it would blow! Now get in the truck," ordered Sam just as the police car appeared behind the store and drove over to block the truck from backing out.

"Hey, what do you think you're doing?" Sam yelled.

"Oh, it's you Mr. Hawkins," Deputy Stan said as he approached the truck.

"We're just checking on a citizen's report about illegal dynamite in the area."

"Well I'm in a hurry so if you don't mind moving your squad car..."

"What's under the tarp?"

"Just some supplies I have to deliver," Sam quickly replied.

"You mind if I take a look?"

"Yeah I do!" Sam yelled.

"Since we have a direct witness report on the dynamite, I have the right to check," said Deputy Stan pulling back the tarp.

"Well, well, it looks like four boxes of dynamite to me. Would both of you please get out of the truck and put your arms on the side of it," he ordered as the other officer stepped forward to frisk, and then handcuff both men.

"You're making a big mistake," Sam yelled. "I have a permit to sell dynamite."

"Do you have a special permit which I've never heard of before, to store it in a commercial area in this town?" Deputy Stan asked.

There was no response from Sam or Phil as the deputy put both men in his squad car. The other officer called the bomb disposal unit to come out and pick up the four boxes as well as check the hardware store for more dynamite. Within a few minutes another police car appeared to watch the dynamite and truck as Deputy Stan drove Sam and Phil to the police station.

"Well I'd say we did a rather good job of stopping them from blowing up the cavern," Jonathan said with a smile.

"Without the dynamite and now watched by the police, they'll have a hard time bothering us for a while," Nicholas replied.

"Should we go to the station and check on

Mikaia?" asked Jonathan.

"I don't think so. The last thing I heard before meeting you was Deputy Stan asking her to wait for a while. After catching Sam and Phil in the act with the dynamite, he'll probably let her leave when he returns. I'm sure she'll come right back to her room, so let's wait for her there." Jonathan nodded at Nicholas as they both made the hand-slide sign and disappeared.

"Thanks for waiting," Deputy Stan said to Mikaia as he led Sam and Phil through the station. "You did a great service to the community. Dynamite in town is very dangerous to everyone, Thanks! If you want to leave you may."

"So, it was you who sent the police! I should have known. But how did you know what we were going to do?" Sam asked with a curious yet hostile look on his face.

"We know about most of the things you're planning to do. Until you and your friends stop interfering in our activities, we'll interrupt yours and stop you from hurting anyone!" replied Mikaia hoping she was vague enough that Deputy Stan wouldn't understand.

Both Sam and Phil looked at each other and frowned as they were led back to the processing room.

"Great, then everything went as planned for you?" Jonathan asked as they heard a soft pop and saw

Mikaia standing in her room.

"Deputy Stan brought them both in and booked them. I was surprised, but glad to see Phil Steward with him. They were not very happy, but they will probably be out on bail tomorrow morning. I'm sure that with this charge they won't be doing anything illegal to stop us for a long time," Mikaia replied.

"Why are you so sure of that?" asked Jonathan.

"I had a nice talk with the deputy sitting at the front desk," she replied with a big smile.

Chapter Thirteen

The Search

"This instant time traveling is awesome," Jonathan said. It's better than cell phones if we need to communicate."

"We have to be careful how and when we use the hand-slide sign. We should probably get cell phones for plain communicating," Mikaia said.

"Do you think Mom and Dad would let us each have one?" Jonathan asked.

"Maybe. We could ask, at least. You have to remember that today we could have used them because we were all sliding at the same time in the same town. If we were to time travel to a distant place, or time travel to a different time, they wouldn't work. So, we can only use them around here, just like everyone else," Nicholas said.

"We really wouldn't need them, then," said Mikaia.

"They'd still be handy like when we called Dad, using Mom's cell, the other night from Ashlee's house," replied Jonathan.

"Hey, are all of you still in Mikaia's room?" their

mom asked, knocking on the door.

"Yes Mom, we're still in here," Mikaia said as she opened the door.

"You've been in there a long time. Are you planning the invasion of a foreign country?"

"No Mom, just talking about Ashlee's party and stuff," replied Mikaia.

"This phone call is for the three of you," Mom said as she handed the phone to Mikaia.

"Hello, this is Mikaia. Oh, 'Hi,' Larry...tomorrow you, Will, Ashlee and Marie want to show us all the hangouts around Opportunity?...And your brother, Mike, who's hasn't left for college yet, promised to drive us around in your Dad's Suburban? Sounds great. Let me check with Nicholas and Jonathan and my Mom. Could you hold on for a moment?"

"How does that sound? They want to show us around tomorrow and Ashlee's older brother will take us," said Mikaia.

"Sound's great to me!" said Jonathan.

"Me too, besides we could use a break, and if we're driving we won't have to worry about having to dance," replied Nicholas.

Mikaia quickly disappeared downstairs to check with their mom. After a couple of minutes, she came back up.

"Larry, sorry to make you wait. It sounds good to us, thanks. You'll probably pick us up at our ranch at eleven? You have to double check with Mike when he gets back since he's taken Ashlee and Marie for a promised hike near May Lake in Yosemite today? Sure, if the time changes, just give us a call. We'll be ready. Bye!"

"This is great! Now we get a chauffeured tour of the area," said Jonathan.

"And get to know some friends," added Mikaia.

"You know, for some reason I feel that we're not going to be able to go on a tour tomorrow. Instead we'll be doing something else," Nicholas said with a thoughtful look on his face.

"What do you mean?" asked Mikaia.

"I don't know, I can't explain it," Nicholas replied.

"You just worry too much," replied Jonathan.

"By the way, Mom says to plan on dinner in about an hour. I'm going to help her," said Mikaia hurrying down the stairs.

"I'm going to try and work it out so I can sit next to Marie tomorrow in the Suburban...She's kinda cute," Jonathan said.

"That will probably leave me near Ashlee, and that would be okay too," Nicholas replied as they both smiled.

"Hello? Yes, Pete?" a female voice said. "You're on your way down to the Sheriff's Office to make bail for whom? Sam and Phil? I don't care if they're going to pay you back. What happened?"

As she continued to speak, her voice became more

agitated and shrill.

"You say that Sam called? And said the Sheriff caught him and Phil loading dynamite at the back of the store? As he was leaving to blow up the cavern? Mikaia Frazier tipped them off? How did they...? Possession and transportation of a dangerous substance within the city? I can't believe this! Okay, take care of them and we'll all meet later."

As the furious female voice slammed down the phone, she added, "I can't believe the trouble those three kids have caused!"

At dinner Jonathan asked his dad if they could have cell phones.

"Do you think you actually need them?" his dad replied.

"They would let us all communicate with each other," Jonathan said, "like if I had to stay after school for football practice, or Mikaia had a class meeting..."

"Or we needed a ride home, or the three of us needed to touch bases with each other about something...," Nicholas added.

"I can see they'd be useful, but it would be expensive for us to have five phones. Do you know what the middle school policy is for students having and using them on campus?" their dad asked.

"I guess we'll have to check about that. I'll ask our friends tomorrow," Mikaia replied just as the phone rang.

"I'll get it," Mikaia said since she was seated closest to the ringing phone.

"Oh, hi Larry. What's the matter? She's what? How did...they're searching for her now. Her parents are driving up and her brother is going back up in the morning if they haven't found her tonight. Can we help look if the forest rangers can't find her? If it's necessary a lot of friends are planning to go up tomorrow to help look for her and we could come. When did Mike see she was missing...just at the base of Mount Hoffmann north of May Lake around three?...Well plan on picking us up early tomorrow on your way up if they don't find her tonight. They'll probably have to call the search off soon because of darkness? Please let us know. Thanks, bye."

"We heard most of that, Mikaia. What's wrong?" her mother asked.

"Ashlee's brother, Mike, had taken Ashlee and Marie for a planned hike up Mount Hoffmann in Yosemite this morning since Ashlee likes to hike in the mountains. On their way back, around three, Mike looked back on the trail and saw Marie but Ashlee wasn't behind them. Marie, who was in front of Ashlee had just talked to her a little while before. So they retraced their steps on the trail and searched for an hour, but couldn't find her.

"They hiked out to the Suburban thinking she might be there, but she wasn't. Mike called the forest rangers and one of their search units met them and is still searching. Mike called home and drove Marie back down. Ashlee's parents drove up to help and Mike plans on bringing friends up tomorrow to help if they haven't found her," Mikaia explained.

"That's terrible!" their dad said. "Maybe we should help look tomorrow too."

"I told them that the three of us would go if Mike drove us back up with him," Mikaia said.

"Then let's see how it goes. You'll need to be careful and stick together and do what the rangers ask if you do go up. I just hope Ashlee survives the night. At nine thousand feet it can get freezing cold, even in the summers," their dad said.

After dinner the triplets met again in Mikaia's room which always seemed the most convenient.

"Wow, this is terrible. I hope they can find her tonight or we can help find her tomorrow," Mikaia said.

"You know Nicholas was right when he said that we wouldn't be going on a tour of Opportunity. We may be going to Yosemite," Jonathan said. "How'd you know?"

"I'm not sure. I just felt that something would happen," Nicholas said.

"Do you think that was what Halo was talking about, the gift of insight we were given?" Jonathan replied.

"I don't know, but I felt really sure about it,"

Nicholas said.

"Mikaia, what are you doing?" Jonathan asked when he saw Mikaia sitting with her eyes closed.

"I just saw someone walking through the forest along a small stream. It was getting dark and she looked worried," Mikaia said.

"Do you think you saw, Ashlee?" Nicholas asked.

"Maybe I was just remembering one of the hikes our family took in Yosemite. We really need to do something right now," Mikaia said.

"Then let's do it right now and time our trip for around two forty-five today. That way we can follow Ashlee on the trail and see what happens to her, but we can't let anyone see us," Nicholas said.

"Great idea! We can lead the rangers to her tomorrow without letting them know what we know," Jonathan replied.

"I'm concerned about her having to spend the night out in the freezing cold," Mikaia said.

"We can't let her see us or we'll have no way of explaining how we found her, much less how we got there," Nicholas said.

"I'll bring an extra coat for the cold and put some matches and a flashlight in the pocket and place it on the trail so she can find it!" Mikaia said. Then she started downstairs to get some matches.

"I like that plan. I'll get my trail map of Yosemite from my room," said Jonathan running out.

As he spread out the trail map, Jonathan asked

Mikaia to tell them exactly what Larry had told her.

"Mike told him that Ashlee disappeared at the base of Mount Hoffmann just north of May Lake about three," Mikaia said as they all looked down at the map and found Mount Hoffmann and May Lake.

"Here's the trail between May Lake and Mount Hoffmann. We'll need to appear at this spot just at the base of the mountain at about two forty-five, hide in the trees, and watch them go by. Then we'll follow them from a distance and see where Ashlee goes," Jonathan suggested. "Are we all together on this?"

"I'm ready," Nicholas said.

"Me too," said Mikaia as she took a coat out of her closet, grabbed a small flashlight and the book of matches, and put them in the coat's front right pocket.

"We all have to concentrate on this spot on the map and remember to focus on two forty-five this afternoon," said Jonathan. They all made the hand-slide sign and heard three pops.

"I don't think I'm ever going to get used to this," Jonathan exclaimed when they all appeared on a dirt trail below a tall granite topped mountain. "It's so amazing!"

"What a gift!" Nicholas agreed.

"Yeah, but we'd better get behind those trees or rocks. If Mike was right, they should be coming down that trail any...Quick, behind those boulders!" Mikaia whispered as they all moved about thirty feet off the trail behind some granite rocks just as the three hikers appeared up the trial.

"I'm really tired, Ashlee," Marie said. "It was an unbelievable hike and view from the top, but I'm ready for a nap."

"I'm with you on that," Ashlee replied.

"We only have a few more miles before we're at the car," Mike yelled back as they passed the boulders the triplets were hiding behind.

"Let's stay back, just out of sight as we follow them," Mikaia said, and they quietly left their hiding place.

About half a mile later they noticed that Ashlee had slowed down a bit and Marie was about fifty feet in front of her, almost out of sight through the fir trees. They saw Ashlee suddenly stop and look into the woods. The triplets moved a little closer and observed a fawn prancing across the trail just in front of Ashlee. Then it bounded into the woods on her left. Ashlee paused for a moment, turned in the direction of the fawn, and walked slowly into the woods.

The triplets carefully approached the spot where Ashlee left the trail. They could barely see her following the fawn. They followed her for several minutes when she suddenly stopped and started looking around. She turned in several directions to get her bearings back to the trail. Suddenly she looked up at the eleven thousand foot mountain just to the north east of her, smiled and started walking through the forest towards it. Jonathan quickly pulled out the map he'd brought.

"She thinks Tuolumne Peak is Mount Hoffmann and is heading at an angle away from the trail! I don't even see another trail up that direction," Jonathan said as he studied the map.

"At least we know how and why she got lost," Nicholas said as they all quietly followed her from a distance.

After about another twenty minutes Ashlee stopped and again looked around her.

The triplets could make out the fear and concern on her face even from their distant hiding spot. Once more she looked up through the trees. Seeing the top of Tuolumne Peak, she continued to head in the wrong direction.

"Nicholas," Mikaia said, "I'm seeing that stream in the forest again. I see a girl heading towards it. It looks like...Ashlee!"

"Wow," Mikaia, that's amazing," Jonathan said.

"Nicholas, you're the fastest. Could you take this jacket and quickly circle around in front of her and lay it by the stream? I see a small clearing and a grassy area just next to it about a block in front of her," Mikaia asked.

"Sure," Nicholas said. He grabbed the coat and hurried around to his right as he said, "Don't move! I'll meet you right back here by this large granite rock!"

It only took Nicholas about three minutes to move rapidly through the forest. He spotted the clearing just as he saw Ashlee in the woods a-ways behind him. He placed the jacket in the middle of the clearing next to the stream and hurried back into the forest before Ashlee arrived. He could see she had tears in her eyes and was wiping her nose when she came out onto the grassy area. He paused for a moment to watch.

Ashlee slowly walked over to the stream, cupped her hand, bent down and drank some water. She pulled out her empty water bottle and began to fill it. Then she looked around as the shadows in the forest began to lengthen.

After a moment or two Ashlee stood up and noticed the coat lying in the meadow grass about twenty feet to her right. She walked over to it and picked it up. Looking around, apparently for the owner, she put it on, checked the pockets, and pulled out the flashlight and matches. She looked around again with a puzzled look on her face.

Nicholas wished he could go to her and bring her with him, so she wouldn't have to spend the night alone.

As he watched a little longer, he saw her walk back into the woods and bring back some broken branches which she piled in the center of the small meadow clearing. He knew that she would build a fire and spend the night in the clearing by the stream. He paused for another moment then hurried back through the forest retracing his steps.

When he got back to the boulder, Mikaia and Jonathan were waiting. He told them what had happened and that she'd be spending the night by the stream. They agreed to retrace their steps back to the trail watching for land marks so they could lead the rangers to her in the morning.

When they got back to the trail they could hear a distant voice yelling for Ashlee as they all made the hand-slide sign and popped back to Mikaia's room.

"It took all my mental energy to not walk out into the meadow and bring Ashlee out," Nicholas said sitting with his siblings on Mikaia's bed.

"You did the right thing. There is no way you could have explained things. She should be all right now and we know where to find her in the morning. But I do think I'll call Larry and see if everything is set for the tomorrow," Mikaia said as she left the room.

"Having this power is incredible, but it can also make things more difficult for us," said Nicholas.

"We're all going to have to discipline ourselves to make sure we use it at the right time and in the right way to help others and protect the old school," Jonathan replied.

In the morning Mike picked them up at six for the two hour drive up highway 140 then 120 towards Tuolumne Meadows in Yosemite. Larry, Will, and

Calvin were also with him. The drive seemed to take forever before they pulled into the trailhead parking area for May Lake and Mount Hoffmann. Several ranger trucks and an ambulance were also there. One of the rangers approached them.

"We had to call off the search after dark last night, but I've already sent two search parties up the trail early this morning, one with your parents," said Ranger Johnson whom Mike recognized from the day before.

"We want to help too. I know the trail and the area from other hikes I've taken. These are friends of Ashlee who also want to help," Mike said.

"Well, I'm sending two more teams of two rangers each along with some people to assist them. I'll split your group in half and put you with those teams," the ranger said.

"If you don't mind, the three of us would like to stay together," said Nicholas quickly.

"That's fine with me. You can go with Rangers Foley and McNear over there," he said as he pointed. "And Mike, why don't you go with them?"

"Glad to, as long as we can help!"

"And you three young men can help Ranger Kline," Ranger Johnson said to Larry, Will, and Calvin.

"Rangers Foley and McNear, I'm Mike Wilson, Ashlee's brother and these are three of her friends, Nicholas, Jonathan and Mikaia Frazier."

"Nice to meet all of you. We can sure use the help, but you'll need to do what we say and stay relatively close together. We will spread out a bit when we start the search but we will always keep in visual contact. Mike, since you saw your sister last, why don't you take us to where that was? We have it marked on the map from your earlier information but the exact location could make a difference," Ranger Foley said.

"Sure, let's get going. I'm really worried and want to find her as soon as we can," Mike replied as Ranger Foley turned and started up the trail.

Almost two miles up the trail near May Lake they hiked north and then turned west to the base of Mount Hoffmann. Just as the trail started to climb, Mike put his hand up as though to stop them.

"Right here we stopped for a moment and talked. Ashlee was out of water so she drank some of mine. Then we hiked down the trail about a block when I heard the girls talk about being tired. I yelled back that we only had a few miles to go to get back to the Suburban. We hiked less than a mile further when I stopped and turned around for a short rest and saw Marie but not Ashlee," Mike said. Then he led them back to the spot where he had last heard her.

"She disappeared between here and about a mile down the trail. Is that right?" Ranger Foley asked.

"Yes, when I stopped she was gone," Mike said.

"Then let's retrace your steps back along the trail.

"Look! There are several footprints
right here.!

She must have left it for some reason at some

point. We'll put two of us on the right edge of the trail and two on the left. The remaining two will space themselves ten feet into the woods on each side and look for footprints or any sign of someone leaving the trail. We'll do this for the next mile and see what we can find," Ranger Foley said.

"We'll take the left side," Nicholas quickly volunteered.

"Then we'll take the right," Ranger Foley said and they spread out and started down the trail. "Now look for any signs at all that could have been caused by Ashlee. It's really hard to see much on the trail since so many feet have hiked across it this summer, but maybe something will stand out along the edges."

After fifteen minutes they approached the spot where Ashlee had turned off the trail to the left.

"Look!" Nicholas said. "There are several footprints that turn off into the woods right here."

"It looks like they head off in this direction although it's harder to see them once they go off the trail and into the needles and dead branches lying under the trees," Mikaia said.

Ranger Foley came over to check out the footprints. "You're right. Some hikers have left the trail and headed northeast by the way it looks. Ashlee may have been one of them, but it's hard to tell. Hikers often leave the trail for all kinds of reasons. Mike, why don't you go with Nicolas, Jonathan, and Mikaia and check it out? Then return to this spot on the trail. Ranger McNear and I will continue down the trail and search for a single set of tracks that leave it. We'll meet you back here in about forty minutes," said Ranger Foley.

As Mike, Nicholas, Jonathan, and Mikaia walked through the trees, they looked for any signs of Ashlee from the day before.

"Look here, Mike! These needles have been kicked up," Jonathan said.

"You're right. Let's keep going," Mike said.

About a block further it was Nicholas's turn. "Hey, a branch on this small fir tree has been freshly bent and almost broken off!"

"Someone has been moving this direction in the last 24 hours," said Mike even more determined to rush forward.

About a block further Mikaia spoke up. "I think I smell smoke!"

"Mikaia, we're looking for tracks and things," Jonathan said thinking it was silly of her to say she smelled smoke when there wasn't any.

"No, Jonathan, I do smell smoke," she said again. They all stopped and sniffed.

"You're right, Mikaia. I smell some now too! It seems to be drifting through the trees from over that way," Mike said and started walking even faster towards the stream and clearing.

"I hear a stream...and through the trees I see a clearing...and a small fire is burning!...and someone is laying next to it! Ashlee!" Mike yelled. Ashlee slowly sat up and turned around.

"Mike, you found me! How did you know where I was?" she yelled hugging her brother.

"We followed your footprints off the trail until we smelled the smoke from your fire. Are you all right?"

"Yes, I was scared but I stayed by the fire that I had built to keep warm and make a smoke signal. But I guess no one could see it at night. Then I finally fell asleep a little while ago and let it burn down," Ashlee explained.

Upon seeing the triplets, she added, "Hi, Mikaia, Nicholas, and Jonathan, I didn't expect to see you way out here. Thanks for helping to find me!" She gave each of them a hug. Nicholas blushed when he got the longest hug.

"Yeah, they've been a lot of help," Mike said. "By the way, where did you get that coat? You certainly didn't have it on the hike with you yesterday."

"It's the funniest thing. I got lost following a fawn and came to this clearing, where I drank some water from the stream. Then when I looked up, I saw a coat lying on the meadow grass...just lying there. In its pocket were a flashlight and a book of matches! I couldn't have asked for a better gift than that. Of course I wish I'd been found sooner, but..."

"Some hiker came prepared, but it's strange he forgot it in the clearing," said Mike.

"We'd better hurry back to the trail and let Ranger

Foley and all the search parties know we found Ashlee and that she's all right," said Nicholas.

"You're right! Can you walk, Ashlee?" Mike asked.

"I'm a bit stiff but to get home I'd run," she said as she turned and started for the place in the trees from which her rescuers had just appeared.

Back at the trail Ranger Foley and Ranger McNear, were relieved to see Ashlee and her rescuers. After some more hugs and a couple of radio calls to the other search parties, Ashlee explained again what had happened and how she survived the cold night.

At the trail head the ambulance and attendants who had been waiting, just in case they were needed, checked Ashlee's vital signs and said she was fine and free to go home. After more hugs with her parents and thanks to all those who had helped search for her, Ashlee left for home and Mike drove her friends back to Opportunity.

Once in the Suburban, Calvin, Larry and Will wanted to know more about how Mike and the triplets had found Ashlee. The triplets tried to explain carefully. There was a lot of laughing and even singing most of the way home.

Chapter Fourteen

Terry

The triplets' parents were anxious to hear what had happened and relieved to find out that Ashlee was fine. After giving them all the details, the triplets went up to Mikaia's room and collapsed on the bed.

"I'm sure glad everything turned out the best way possible. Ashlee is fine and she stayed by the fire waiting to be found instead of wandering further off," Jonathan said.

"And no one knows how we really helped find her," said Nicholas.

Mikaia sat up and hurried towards her closet. After looking in her closet for a moment and pulling out a couple of jackets Mikaia's face seemed to turn white.

"So, what's the matter? You have to be happy about finding Ashlee?" Jonathan asked.

"I think I really slipped up," replied Mikaia.

"In what way?" asked Nicholas.

"The jacket I grabbed to take for her was one Mom gave me to take to school on cold and rainy days in San Francisco," she replied.

216

"So, Mom won't see her wearing it," said Jonathan.

"Probably not, but I forgot that Mom had written my name on the label tag in case I misplaced the coat at school!" At that point both the boys were sitting up. "What if she sees it?" Mikaia said.

"How do we explain that coincidence?" Jonathan asked. "Speaking of some fast talking!"

"You know one of us could pop into her room tonight and take it back," Nicholas suggested.

"That's too risky. She might see us. Then we'd really have a problem!" Mikaia said.

"Besides, she may have already seen your name in the coat, so we should decide what we should say if she has," Jonathan said.

"You're right," returned Mikaia.

They both looked over at Nicholas who had a strange smile on his face. As they stared at him he looked up and asked, "Do you remember the things we took to the Salvation Army donation center just outside of town when we first moved into Opportunity?"

"I do. I remember Mom and Dad telling us to donate anything we had out grown or didn't plan on using," Jonathan answered.

"Well, I think it was sure nice of Mikaia to have donated the warm coat that someone must have bought to go hiking in," Nicholas said with an even bigger smile.

"Good idea, Nicholas!" Mikaia said.

"Yeah, but what are the odds of that happening?" asked Jonathan.

"In a small community like Opportunity, I'd say pretty good. At least it's a believable story," Nicholas returned.

"Then that's what I'll say if Ashlee asks me. What else could she believe?" Mikaia said with a relieved grin. "But I must say that I don't like bending the truth about the coat."

"In a way you did donate it, didn't you? Instead of giving it to the Salvation Army you left it in a meadow for someone to find who really needed it," Jonathan said.

"I guess it was a donation if you look at it that way. But I still don't like to mislead people," Mikaia replied

"In our case we're going to have to mislead people when it comes to our powers and how we use them, otherwise we won't be able to use them to help anyone," said Nicholas. "In every other way we'll always tell the truth. Truth and trust go together so we must be truthful in order to build and keep the trust of our family and friends whenever we can."

"You're right, although with our powers it can be harder for us than other truthful people," replied Mikaia.

"Speaking of powers, both of you seem to have found some very helpful ones when we needed them, just like Halo said," Jonathan mentioned.

"What do you mean?" asked Nicholas.

"Mikaia was able to have a vision of where Ashlee was going to be and even the meadow clearing by the stream where she told you to place the coat. You were able to determine the future by knowing that we'd not be going on a tour of Opportunity but instead doing something else. I think Halo called it a kind of intuition or insight. He said we'd each discover our gifts when we needed them," Jonathan said.

"You're right. I guess we do have those gifts," Mikaia agreed.

"Yeah, you do but I don't," complained Jonathan.

"Halo said we all had this power so you'll just have to discover yours at the right time," said Nicholas.

"I still think he made a mistake about me having that kind of power," Jonathan replied sadly.

"You'll find it, Jonathan," said Mikaia as she gave him a pat on the back.

"I hope it's in time to help us stop the Followers from destroying the old school's powers and even the old school," Jonathan said.

"I've been thinking about that," Nicholas said. "I'm worried that when Sam and Phil are out on bail they or other Followers will try to blow up the cavern again and destroy the machine. Sam Hawkins might be so mad that he just doesn't care if he gets caught and goes to jail."

"I think we should take a trip into town tomorrow

and visit the hardware store to see how he and Evelyn are doing," Mikaia suggested.

"You sure are brave going to see Sam, now that he knows you're the one who told the sheriff about him," Jonathan said.

"I'm not afraid of him, just cautious. I would like to get his reaction so we can figure out what his next move could be," replied Mikaia.

"You've got a good point, Mikaia. We need to figure out what the Followers are going to do before they do it, if we can," Nicholas added. "Besides, I want to check out the antique shop again. Since we got our allowance for chores and things, I think I have enough to buy one of the old mining camp whisky bottles that Terry has in the store."

"And I could look at any new documents she has and of course afterwards end up at the ice cream shop!" Jonathan replied.

"I've got an idea," Mikaia said. "I'll call Ashlee and see if she and Marie would like to meet us at the Café and Grill for lunch and of course some ice cream for dessert. That way we can see how she's doing after all this."

"Great, a trip to town! We can size up Sam Hawkins, peruse the antique shop, have lunch and ice cream with friends. I like that!" Jonathan added.

"Speaking of chores, I have a few more to do tonight," Mikaia said.

"Me too," Nicholas returned. "I've got to sweep

out the garage and sweep off the porch."

"How about you, Jonathan?" asked Mikaia.

"Yeah, I've got a job too, again," he said with a frown.

"Well what is it?" asked Nicholas as Jonathan looked down. "Not Spiderman again? Man! Dad must think you do a great job of knocking down all those webs in the garage and barn!"

He couldn't help but laugh.

"Don't laugh too loud, Nicholas," Jonathan said. "I plan to start knocking down the spiders in the garage as soon as I see you come in with the broom to sweep!"

"Then I'll just wait until sometime late tonight to do it!" replied Nicholas.

"Then I'll just keep an eye out down the hall to see when you leave!" returned Jonathan.

"Boys!" Mikaia exclaimed as she left her room to call Ashlee and Marie.

In the morning the triplets finished their chores, along with a few others Dad saved for them, before heading into town. They decided to ride their bikes since their mom and dad were still busy with the chores they had assigned to themselves. "Everyone works on a ranch," their parents had said as the triplets rode off.

They parked their bikes in front of the hardware store. After taking a deep breath to get their courage up, they walked in. Behind the counter they saw Sam

Hawkins who looked at them as though he would charge at them any minute.

"I didn't think you'd have the courage to come into my store so soon after what you did to me," he snarled.

"You did it to yourself, Mr. Hawkins. You stored dangerous materials in town that could have hurt many people. We were just doing our civic duty and saving you from a possible manslaughter charge if any of it had gone off and killed someone," Mikaia said pleasantly.

"I know what you were really trying to do and that was to save your powers from being blown up! You can't fool me! You're all going to have to learn to mind your own business," Sam replied.

"You know that we will still try to protect the old school and we'll do anything to stop you. If you just leave us and the old school alone, we'll all get along just fine," Mikaia answered back.

"We've all got our jobs to do and I know what mine is!" Sam replied.

"That's too bad. We'd hoped we could work something out and be civil to each other," Mikaia returned as Sam tried to stare her down.

"It won't make any difference if you and the other Followers meet tonight to plan your next move against us, Mr. Hawkins," Jonathan found himself saying.

"How did you know that that's what I was just

thinking, boy?" a surprised Sam quickly asked.

"Well...I just sort of thought that's what you were thinking," replied a surprised Jonathan.

"You may know some things but you don't know the important stuff," Sam snarled back.

"You mean that you're planning to get Mr. Steward to go back in the tunnel with you tomorrow night with some dynamite that you're going to pick up in Mariposa this afternoon?" replied Jonathan, amazed at himself.

"Boy, what are you, some kind of weird mind reader or something?" Sam grunted as a hint of fear appeared on his face.

"We told you earlier that we know what you and your friends are going to do as soon as you do. So why don't you just stop trying to hurt others and concentrate on running your business?" Mikaia replied.

A very frustrated Sam looked at the triplets and told them that if they weren't going to buy anything right now, they should leave his store.

"We hope you have a nice day, Mr. Hawkins," Mikaia said as they started to leave.

Jonathan couldn't keep himself from saying, "At least a day a little better than yesterday."

"I don't think he's going to stop until he destroys the old school and runs us out of town," Jonathan said. "I was so mad that I couldn't help but rub it in a bit."

"We found out one thing, that's for sure," Nicholas said.

"Isn't it obvious, Jonathan?" Mikaia added.

"What's obvious?" Jonathan replied.

"You discovered your gift when you needed it," Nicholas said.

"Yeah, I was wondering about that. Those thoughts just came to my mind as I looked at Sam and I decided to say what I was thinking," said Jonathan with a smile.

"I think your gift is the ability to read minds, Jonathan. You seemed to be right on and that frustrated the heck out of Sam," Nicholas replied.

"Maybe you're right. I do have a gift and that could be it!" Jonathan said enthusiastically.

"A gift you're going to have to use wisely. You could find out things you really don't want to know. You'd better learn when to turn it off and on. It could cause you a lot of trouble and worry," Mikaia said.

"But it could be very helpful to us as we try to save the old school and help others, if it's used right," Nicholas added.

"Yeah, I'm going to have to figure this out and try to learn to control it," Jonathan said.

"After all that fun, let's check out the antique store. Besides we have fifteen minutes before we meet Ashlee and Marie at the Café and Grill for lunch," Mikaia said.

"And ice cream," Jonathan added.

"Yes, and ice cream for dessert, Jonathan," Mikaia said shaking her head.

As they entered the antique shop Terry looked over and smiled. "Back again. Are you looking for anything special that I can help you with?"

"I want to look at your old bottles again," Nicholas said.

"And I want to see if you have any new, but old documents," Jonathan added.

"I did get a hold of some more old land deeds and mining ledgers where they kept track of their expenses," Terry replied.

"Great!" Jonathan said. "I'll look through them."

Nicholas decided to show one of the mining bottles he was planning on buying to Mikaia.

"Now this one I really like. It's about a hundred and fifty years old, but I can buy it for my collection for thirty dollars," he said as he handed it to Mikaia.

"It looks like it was hand blown and I like the dark brown color," she said as she handed it back. Nicholas reached out for it but it slipped from his hand and shattered on the floor.

Within a second Terry was there.

"What did you do?" she cried out in a high-pitched voice. "You broke one of my bottles!"

"You careless boy!" she shrieked.

"I'm awfully sorry, I didn't mean to drop such an important bottle," Nicholas stammered back.

"Well you did," Terry replied as she began to calm

down.

"I'll be happy to pay for it. I have the money since I was planning to buy it today anyway," Nicholas returned.

By now Terry had calmed down to what seemed to be her normal self.

"I realize you didn't mean to drop it, Nicholas. Accidents do happen sometimes," she said.

"I still want to pay for it," said Nicholas.

"Let's compromise then," Terry said. "You pay for the bottle you broke and I'll let you pick out another bottle of lesser value to add to your collection. Do we have a deal?" she asked.

Nicholas, who thought that was more than fair, smiled and said, "Deal!"

He reached in his pocket and handed Terry the thirty dollars he'd saved for the bottle.

"Now you may pick out any bottle for your collection from this row," Terry said and pointed to some less expensive bottles.

Nicholas picked out a nice old medicine bottle that was also hand blown with a dark blue color and thanked Terry as they left the antique shop.

"Man, Nicholas, you've got to be more careful. You really made Terry upset," Jonathan said.

"I certainly didn't mean to drop the bottle or upset her,' Nicholas replied.

"Actually, it was a good thing you did," Mikaia said.

"What do you mean?" asked Nicholas.

"You were so busy feeling guilty about dropping the bottle you missed her shrieking voice," Mikaia said.

"Yes, that noise did sound kind of familiar," said Jonathan.

"Familiar all right!" Nicholas said. "That's the female voice we heard in the tunnel!"

"And from the cavern when we hid under the invisible shield," said Jonathan.

"I'm afraid Terry is the leader of the Followers!" Mikaia said.

"I never would have thought that was possible," said Jonathan. "She even sold us the Timber Pine Mine Claim we so badly needed after Miss Ivy couldn't find it. That's why we thought Miss Ivy might have been a Follower."

"Terry is the one who told us Miss Ivy was looking for it. She probably did that to throw us off," Nicholas said, "and to set us up for Ned Steward when we went back looking for Jonathan. Maybe he was supposed to push us all into the mine shaft!"

I can't believe that a seemingly nice lady is the most evil of the Followers and a right hand of Cryptic!" replied Mikaia.

"His Followers normally do try to blend in. It's easier for them to gather recruits that way. They spoil you with supposed friendship, lure you in, then take over," Nicholas said.

"It's hard to understand how people can be so gullible to the point where they do evil things too," remarked Jonathan.

"Cryptic must find it very easy with the number of Followers he seems to have. Look at the Followers he has just in the small town of Opportunity," Nicholas added as they walked into the Café and Grill.

"Hi Ashlee!" Mikaia said walking over to her and giving her a hug. "How are you feeling?"

"Well, I kind of miss the dark lonely nights, alone in an unknown forest, but other than that, fine," she said with a smile as they all laughed.

"I still can't get over the fact I didn't look back for almost a mile to talk to Ashlee. If I had, we would have stopped sooner and maybe found her," Marie said. "I must have been really tired!"

"And I still can't believe I left the trail to follow a fawn! I've never done that before," Ashlee replied.

"You must have been tired too and not acting like you normally would," Nicholas said.

"I really appreciate what the three of you did. Mike told me that you were the ones to pick up on my trail and encourage him to go that direction," Ashlee continued, "and especially you, Mikaia."

"Why especially me?" asked Mikaia.

"We'll talk later," she replied as they all picked up a menu and ordered.

"We still need to take the three of you on a tour. Ashlee said that Mike would be in town for another week before leaving to get set up at his college, and he is still willing to take us around," Marie announced.

"We'd like that," said Jonathan. He quickly turned the menu over looking for the desserts.

"Then how about the day after tomorrow?" asked Ashlee.

"Fine with me," Mikaia said as Jonathan and Nicholas looked up from the burgers they had ordered and nodded.

After some ice cream and goodbyes, the triplets headed out to their bikes for the ride home.

"I'm glad Ashlee's all right, but I'm a bit worried about her wanting to talk to me later about something. She may have found the tag with my name on it," Mikaia said as they pushed their bikes down the street.

"If that's the case then you tell her about the donation, that's all," Nicholas said.

"Yeah, I know, but it's still difficult."

"What's difficult is that Sam's still planning to blow up the cavern tomorrow night," Jonathan noted.

"He might not do it now, since you told him you knew about it," said Mikaia.

"Or," Nicholas replied, "he may think that he should do it anyway since we wouldn't expect it because we knew he was going to do it."

"Wow, I think I followed you on that, Nicholas," said Jonathan. "So where does that leave us?"

"It means that tomorrow we'd better check the tunnel and cavern," Nicholas replied.

Then they all hopped on their bikes and started up the long hill towards their ranch.

Chapter Fifteen

Rebellion

The sun was just going down when the back door to the storage room of the hardware store flew open. Sam and Evelyn, along with Phil and Mabel were waiting inside.

"Where's Pete Rider?" Terry said storming into the room.

"I'm right behind you," Pete said following her in.

"Something's got to be done about those triplets! They're in way over their heads," exclaimed Terry.

"Maybe we're the ones in over our heads when it comes to them and their powers," Phil Steward said.

"What do you mean by that?" Terry asked curtly.

"It seems to me that every time we've planned to do something, they've stopped us. We couldn't keep them away from the old school when Pete tried to buy it because of their presentation to the school board. They threatened to expose Pete to the community and time traveled back to see him as a boy. Sam's grandson got scared away when he tried to guard the playground and I still think they had something to do with that. Sam's grandfather snatched one of them when they traveled back in time but they were able to save him plus eliminate Ned Hawkins. Recently they were able to find out about the dynamite at Sam's hardware store and have the sheriff arrive just as we had loaded it up. Now Sam and I are set up with possible jail time. I think their powers have grown to the point that only Cryptic can beat them," Phil replied.

"I'm still for trying to destroy their powers and taking back control of things around here, however..." Sam said as he was cut off.

"However, what? You're afraid to?" an angry Terry bleated out.

"Now one of them can read minds!" Sam stammered out.

"Can what? How do you know?" asked Terry.

"When they came into my store today one of them, Jonathan, told me that I planned to go to Mariposa this afternoon and pick up more dynamite. Then Phil and I will use it on the old school tomorrow night. As you all know, that's exactly what we planned to do!"

"It might have been just a lucky guess. They knew you'd need more dynamite if you were to destroy the tunnel," replied Terry trying to dispel any worry.

"Yeah, but he also told me that he knew we were going to meet tonight to plan our next move...another lucky guess?" Sam asked.

"It looks like the Master Inventor has promoted

them to a higher status. Now they may be as dangerous to us as Halo," Terry said deep in thought.

"Jonathan was wrong about one thing," Phil said. "I'm not going back in that tunnel to blow anything up. Matter of fact, Mable and I plan to retire from everything. We've done our share over the years."

"What was that?" said Terry suddenly.

"What do you mean?" Sam replied.

"I thought I heard something back along the wall by the shelves."

"I've had this place locked tight all day. It probably was a rat. I've had some problems with them lately."

"I agree with Phil," Pete added. I've done more than my share over the years and I can't afford to have any more trouble around here if I'm planning on staying."

"That's the way Mable and I feel," Phil added. "I still face some possible jail time."

They could see Terry's face turn red and knew what was coming.

"You don't come and go as you please! Once you become a Follower of Cryptic you're always a Follower of Cryptic. He's the one who decides whether you've done enough or should be eliminated! You have no choice in the matter!" she yelled out. "We still have work to do!"

"You still have work to do, not us! If we can't live our lives peacefully in the community in which we were raised, we might as well, as you say, be eliminated. I don't see what good that would do you or Cryptic. The pioneer families Steward and Rider disappear from Opportunity after living here since the 1850's! You don't think that headline would get some major attention from the sheriff, the neighboring police. and possibly the FBI? They'd be all over this town for months turning over every rock to figure things out," Phil replied.

Terry's angry stare was directed at Phil then Pete. Her mouth curled up as she said, "Then eliminated it will be!"

"Not without Cryptic's consent," Phil said. "And I for one don't think he wants to have his power in the area and over other Followers negated while authorities look at things around here that he doesn't want revisited, just to get rid of us. I'm betting our lives on it!"

"That you are!" Terry said. "I can't believe that three kids are your downfall!"

"Not just kids, but the Frazier kids and their powers. That makes a big difference!" Pete replied.

"Then Sam and I will take care of things while Cryptic decides what to do with you!" Terry replied.

"Accidentally the Frazier triplets will be caught in a mine tunnel cave-in. These tunnels are old and sections collapse all the time. That way most of our problems will be solved and we can focus on recruiting more Followers for Cryptic!" she added.

"That is if Cryptic approves it!" Pete said.

"Not only has Cryptic approved it, he plans on helping us make sure the triplets are gone!" Terry exclaimed triumphantly, while the others gasped.

"He's even given me the only complete copy of a map with all the mining tunnels ever dug around here to help us plan the triplets' little surprise!'"

In the morning the triplets decided to check out the old school and cavern to make sure they hadn't been tampered with the previous night. Sam had told them he 'had a job to do' so they knew they needed to check on things, often.

"You know we could just use the hand-slide signal to appear in the cavern this morning," Jonathan reminded Nicholas and Mikaia as they started down the stairs to eat breakfast.

"That should only be used for important trips. Besides I can use the exercise of tramping through some tunnels this morning," Nicholas replied.

"I agree," Mikaia chimed in. "We should use that power only when there is no other way."

"Hi kids. How was your trip to town yesterday?" their dad asked.

"Fine, we had a chat with Mr. Hawkins. Then we saw Terry at the antique store where Nicholas bought an old medicine bottle for his collection. After that we had lunch with Ashlee and Marie at the Café and Grill," Mikaia replied.

"How is Ashlee getting along?" their mother

asked as she placed a large plate of pancakes on the table and watched as Nicholas and Jonathan tried to see who could get to it first.

"Hey Jonathan, you've got half of mine too," Nicholas yelled out.

"There are more. Stab another," Jonathan replied.

"Boys!" Mikaia exclaimed. "There's plenty for everyone."

"She's doing fine," Nicholas answered with a mouth full of pancake.

"She can't believe she was that careless to wander off after a fawn," Mikaia added.

"But she's doing well and still wants Mike to take us on that trip around town to show us all the sixth grader hangouts tomorrow."

"That sounds like a good idea," their mom replied.

"What do you plan to do today?" their dad asked.

"We thought we'd go to the creek then follow it down and through the south end of town to where it meets the North Fork of the Merced River. Then we thought we'd have a picnic lunch," Jonathan said.

"That sounds like fun," their mom said. "Would you like me to make some sandwiches for you?"

"Ah, sure Mom, and I'll help," said Mikaia. Then she turned to Jonathan and Nicholas who were finishing off their pancakes, and suggested, "Let's meet in my room in a few minutes."

"Why did you say we were going on a hike and picnic, Jonathan?" asked Mikaia a few minutes later in her room.

"We had to say something. We couldn't say we were going back into the tunnel to check on the time machine! Besides, a picnic sounds fine to me," Jonathan replied.

"I don't like to mislead them either, but we were kind of trapped by Dad's question," Nicholas explained.

"Okay then, I have the sandwiches in my backpack," Mikaia said.

"And I have some flashlights, fishing line, and nails in mine, just in case we want to set some traps," replied Nicholas as they walked down the stairs. "I do have a strange feeling about the cavern."

"Is it a bad feeling?" asked Jonathan.

"No, it's more like something unusual is going to happen," Nicholas replied.

They walked out towards the creek then circled around back into the barn and up into the loft. They climbed down the ladder into the dark tunnel.

"I'm getting used to this tunnel thing," Jonathan said as they hurried along.

"Keep your eyes and ears open. Sam could even be in here now," Nicholas said.

They passed the tunnel that crossed theirs and headed up to where the Hole in the Mountain Mine tunnel came in. At the invisible curtain, Nicholas, carefully peeked into the cavern before they entered to be sure none of the Followers were there before them.

"This place is more amazing each time I see it!" Jonathan exclaimed. "It must have taken months to wire all the quartz that lines the cavern wall together and a much longer time to build the machine."

"I still don't know how they did it, especially build the machine," Nicholas added as he pushed through the invisibility shield that covered it.

"Nothing looks like it's been tampered with, and I don't see any explosives in the cavern or near the machine," Mikaia said.

"I don't think anyone's been back, yet!" said Jonathan.

Just as he finished his sentence a loud hum could be heard coming from the machine. The triplets quickly jumped back out through the shield as the quartz began to glow with the brightness of a thousand light bulbs. They tried to cover their ears as the noise became louder. The time machine started to vibrate violently then spin as the invisible shield flapped up and down.

"What's going on here?" yelled Jonathan.

"I'm not sure but I think someone must be time traveling!" Nicholas yelled back.

"Look under the flapping invisibility shield on the machine," said Mikaia. "The magnets are spinning so fast that smoke is coming out into the cavern!"

"That's not smoke. It looks like...cotton candy!" Jonathan exclaimed.

"That crackling electrical sound is awfully loud. Protect your ears and let's get out of the cavern and into the tunnel, quick," yelled Nicholas. The triplets ran over to the far wall and out through the invisible curtain into the tunnel.

The noise in the tunnel was just a hum and the triplets could still feel a mild vibration. All of a sudden the noise and vibration stopped. The triplets stood there in disbelief.

"Someone was time traveling. They had to be! That was just like when we traveled but louder!" Jonathan said. "We're the only ones who time travel, aren't we?"

"I guess not!" Nicholas said. "Let's go back in and check out the machine."

"Look, there is still some of that cotton candy stuff floating around," Jonathan said as he scooped some up, licked it with his tongue, and immediately spit it out. "That's it for sure. Tastes like oil!"

"The machine is still warm but everything else seems quiet," said Mikaia.

"So that's how the machine must cause a slipping and bending of time that lets us take field trips," Nicholas said.

"I'd like to know who was taking one," said Jonathan.

"Me too," Nicholas exclaimed. He shot up the

tunnel leading to the old school with Mikaia and Jonathan close behind.

Once up the ladder he ran through the school to the window that looked out over the playground as the other two crowded in behind him.

"We know one thing. It wasn't a kid who traveled. I see the dust from a car disappearing down the road, but I can't make it out," Nicholas said.

"I wonder where they traveled," pondered Jonathan.

"Could have been anywhere, I guess," Mikaia replied.

"This is really strange. I thought Halo said we were the only ones who have been able to time travel for a long time," Nicholas said.

"Apparently not!" Jonathan replied.

"At least we know no one has damaged the machine. It seems to work very well," Nicholas said.

"Let's leave a few trip lines in the tunnels and cavern on our way back and take that hike and picnic down the creek to the river," Jonathan suggested.

"I'm game!" replied Nicholas.

"Let's get going then. When we come back I want to check out the trunks in the attic, again," Mikaia said.

"Why the trunks, since we've already looked all through them?" Jonathan asked.

"Maybe now that our powers have grown, and we've learned more, some of the stuff may ring a bell with one of us," Mikaia said.

"I'm sure it won't hurt to take another look," agreed Nicholas.

"You know, Nicholas, you were right again," said Jonathan, "about knowing that something strange was going to happen in the cavern today."

"I know. I was just thinking about that," replied Nicholas.

"That's what reminded me of it," Jonathan said as they all looked at each other.

After a pleasant hike to the river and a sandwich or two, they watched as a couple of fishermen floated by in a canoe. Then they headed back home.

"You know Nicholas, football practice starts in a few days. That's what Brad Owens told me. I figure it won't hurt to try out for the defense," Jonathan said.

"I know, Calvin told me three times when it starts. For some reason he thinks I'd make a good linebacker, and for some reason, I feel that I would," Nicholas replied.

"Then until soccer season, if both of you try out for the football team, I might as well try out for cheerleader," Mikaia said. "Then at least I could keep an eye on you!"

"Oh, thanks, Mom," Jonathan said with a smile as he and Nicholas laughed.

After checking back in with their mom, the triplets climbed up to the attic for another look in the trunks left by Harold.

"I'm still not sure what we're looking for," Jonathan said as he opened the lid of one of the four trunks.

"We want to find anything that might look like it could tell us something," said Mikaia lifting a lid on another trunk.

Nicholas was already looking through the trunk he had opened. "All these clothes from 1860 to 1930 sure look different from this small pile to the right," he decided as Mikaia peeked over his shoulder.

"They are different. Those look a little newer than these," she said reaching over and grabbing a couple of shirts.

"See, these are made a little differently, more like we make them today," she explained as she held some up.

"I see what you mean," Nicholas said, examining one of the newer ones. "The teacher must have asked the parents to label their kids' clothes with their initials near the collar."

"At least they knew whose they were," Mikaia said and took two from Nicholas. "This one has a B.G. on it and this one a M.W."

"And these have a B.P., a N.F., and a H.L on them," Nicholas said tossing three shirts back into the pile.

"May I see the H.L. shirt?" Mikaia asked.

Nicholas pulled it back out.

"Now I know this couldn't be Harold Lowe's," she

said.

"Harold went to school so long ago his shirt would be made out of canvas," Jonathan said and they all laughed.

"They could be anybody's," Nicholas said as he heard the sound of a bell ring.

"Sounds like you've got hold of an old brass bell, Jonathan," said Mikaia.

"I like the sound. It sure gives me some weird vibrations but it makes me feel happy!" Jonathan said ringing it again.

Suddenly the triplets heard a popping noise and Halo appeared.

"I knew I'd find you here. I heard Jonathan ringing the small brass bell. It gives off a special vibration," Halo said.

"Hi, Halo. We're glad to see you," Mikaia said.

"What about this bell?" asked Jonathan as he rang it again.

"All I can say is that if I were you I'd keep it with me for a while," Halo said smiling.

"Why should I keep it with me?" asked Jonathan.

"You'll know why when the time comes," answered Halo.

"You sure make us go through all kinds of hoops to find things out when you could just tell us," Jonathan said.

"You're learning a lot and gaining more power. Isn't that a good enough reason to let you figure things out for yourselves?" Halo asked.

"For me it is," answered Mikaia. "And I'm really glad you left these trunks full of stuff as clues for us to follow."

"Yes, that is the reason I left them up here in the attic. Don't forget to keep looking in them. You still have more to discover," Halo said.

"Like what?" Jonathan asked.

Halo merely smiled at him and said, "Nice try, Jonathan."

"We were just in the cavern making sure everything was all right when someone time traveled and the whole cavern went crazy!" Nicholas said.

"Yes, I felt its power being used."

"Then there are others who can time travel?" Nicholas asked.

"You're the first to make use of it for a long time. Since you fixed up the merry-go-round, others who once time traveled can make use of it again and that's apparently what happened," Halo said

"Do you know who it was?" asked Mikaia.

"I have my suspicions, but I don't want to share them at this time."

"We found out who the Followers' leader is in Opportunity," Jonathan said.

"Was it Terry?" Halo asked.

"How'd you know?" Jonathan asked.

"I read your mind. Like the three of you, the Master Inventor long ago gave me several special powers," Halo said. "It does surprise me a little that it is Terry. She's always been so helpful and nice to everyone. It just shows you that Cryptic can turn almost anyone."

"Then you probably know that Sam still plans on blowing up the cavern," Jonathan added.

"Yes, I was just told the Followers recently met about it and I came to warn you that they may try to hurt the three of you."

"I thought they couldn't hurt us!" said Mikaia.

"They alone can't because of your caring souls and powers, but working directly with Cryptic they can. He's shown some unusual interest in the three of you. Something tells me he's actually coming here to help! You've apparently become such a nuisance to him he's taken a personal interest. He seldom does this. So you need to stay together, be very careful, and let your powers warn you about anything unusual. Meanwhile, I and others will be watching too," Halo said.

"This is very scary," Mikaia said. "Do you feel we have the ability to deal with all of this?"

"The Master Inventor and I have a lot of confidence in you and your ability to take care of yourselves...and others."

With that the triplets heard a popping noise and Halo was gone.

"I don't like being a target for anyone, much less Cryptic!" Jonathan shared.

"Me neither," said Mikaia. "We'll need to be very careful."

"I'm not sure why, but if Halo thinks I should keep this bell with me, then I'll do it," said Jonathan.

When he slipped the small brass bell into his pocket, it rang one more time.

"Halo said there are still more clues in these trunks. Maybe we should keep looking," said Nicholas.

"If nothing's jumped out at us yet, we might as well take a rest and come back later after we've learned more stuff," Jonathan suggested.

The triplets agreed to check the trunks out again in a few days and then went downstairs to the kitchen.

Chapter Sixteen

Preparation

"Hi Mom," said Mikaia, "Are you still working?"

"I'm working on a big lasagna casserole for dinner. It takes a lot of time but it will provide us with two meals."

"Great, I love your lasagna," Jonathan said.

"By the way Ashlee called for you, Mikaia, while you were out. I took her number and told her you'd call her back."

"Thanks Mom," said Mikaia as she took the number off the counter and headed toward the hall phone a few feet away.

"Hi, is Ashlee in...Yes, Mikaia...thank you Mrs. Wilson...Hi Ashlee. Do you want to meet me today at the Ice Cream and Candy Shop? Sure, how about three? Okay, see you there."

"Was she checking on the time of our tour tomorrow?" Jonathan asked.

"No, she wanted to meet with me at the ice cream shop at three."

"Did she say why?" asked her mother.

"No, probably just to visit," answered Mikaia.

"Visit who?" their dad asked, appearing in the doorway.

"Oh, visit with Ashlee in town at three."

"Sounds fine to me, I could give you a ride down the hill and back. I have some business in town that will take me about thirty minutes, if that works out."

"That would be great!" replied Mikaia.

"I'd like to go in too," Jonathan said.

"And so would I," Nicholas added.

"Then we'll leave in about an hour."

Mikaia, Jonathan, and Nicholas walked out to the front porch and sat down.

"Why do you want to go?" Mikaia asked.

"I'm sure she's going to ask you about the jacket," Nicholas said. "Right when Mom said she called, I knew she had that on her mind. I just thought I'd be around for support if you needed it."

"And I figured it was another good chance to get some ice cream," Jonathan said. "Also, Halo said we should be sure to stick together, especially now."

"I guess you're right about that. Then that's fine, as long as you give Ashlee and me some space," said Mikaia.

Their dad pulled up in front of the Ice cream and Candy Shop right at three. Mikaia walked in and over to Ashlee whom she had seen sitting by herself near the front window. The boys followed her in and took a seat at a small table across the room.

"Hi Ashlee! You have to forgive my brothers.

When they heard I was meeting you here, they figured it was a good time to get some more ice cream," Mikaia said.

"That's fine. I always enjoy seeing them," Ashlee said smiling and waving at Nicholas and Jonathan.

"What did you want to talk to me about?" asked Mikaia.

"I'm not sure how to say this, but I think you had more to do with my rescue than people know."

"What do you mean, Ashlee?" Mikaia asked.

"I found the jacket just when I needed it, along with a flashlight and matches. The jacket has the name Mikaia on the inside tag. At first it was just a strange coincidence. But Mikaia is a very unusual name and the name of one of my friends who just happened to be with the rescue party that led Mike directly to me." Ashlee said.

"Yes, that really was a coincidence, but the jacket was one that I had taken to the Salvation Army as a donation with a lot of other things when we first moved in. I'd forgotten about it. It's incredible that someone would buy it to hike in and then just leave it where you found it," said Mikaia.

"That's what I thought, especially since it had a flashlight and matches in the pocket. I don't know a lot about the mountains but I do know that most people going on a simple day hike don't usually take a flashlight and matches," Ashlee replied.

"I guess you were just lucky then," Mikaia said.

"I'm still not sure what happened. Somehow I know I owe you, and probably your brothers, a big thank you! You three really are going to become my special friends," Ashlee said as she bent over and gave Mikaia a hug.

"Why don't both of you join us here by the window. I think I'll get some ice cream too," Ashlee directed to the boys.

Several minutes later, Nicholas and Jonathan came over and joined them with the hot fudge sundaes.

"So what time tomorrow are we going on this tour?" Jonathan asked.

"Mike and I will pick you up at ten. Marie and Larry are coming too," Ashlee replied.

"It sounds like fun to me," said Nicholas as he placed another spoonful of mostly hot fudge into his mouth.

A few minutes later their dad came through the door and Mikaia quickly introduced him to Ashlee.

"It's nice to put a face with a name, Ashlee," their dad said.

"And I want to thank you for letting them help rescue me the other day. Probably without them I'd still be lost...and cold," she replied.

Two figures, a man and a woman, sat on a bench in the Town Square Park just across the street from the hotel.

"Then it's all set for tomorrow night, Wednesday, right?" asked Sam.

"Yes, Cryptic and some of his closest Followers will be here," Terry replied. "You do know what you're supposed to do?"

"Yeah, and I can't wait. I drove to a friend's in Sacramento and picked up a bunch of those small explosive charges I told you about. Using your map and knowing how the triplets will probably get to the cavern, I'll place them just right tonight. When Cryptic's ready he himself can destroy the triplets along with the cavern!"

"I don't want anything to go wrong. With Cryptic there, we will succeed, but I still want him to think we set things up correctly. So do your job well!" demanded Terry.

"What did he decide to do about Phil and Pete? Does he plan to eliminate them?" Sam asked with a smile.

"Not right now. He feels that all the cave-ins in the area that will happen tomorrow night will be enough excitement for everyone, especially when the triplets get killed in one. He thinks he can use Phil and Pete later. If not, they too will disappear. Right now I've got to move. I just got lucky and saw the Frazier triplets go into the ice cream store. If I time it right I can set them up for tomorrow," she said as she walked towards the ice cream shop.

Just as the triplets and their dad were leaving the shop, Terry walked by.

"Oh, imagine bumping into you today," exclaimed Terry.

"Yes, imagine that," Nicholas said carefully studying her face.

"Oh, Terry, this is out father, Nathan," Mikaia said. "Terry owns the Opportunity Antique shop."

"Nice to meet you, Terry," he said as Terry gave him a rather strange look.

"Have we met before?" she asked.

"We could have. We've been in town for a while and I've even been in the antique shop a couple of times."

"Well you certainly look familiar. By the way, Sam Hawkins told me to tell you something if I happened to see you. You know he has the Hardware Store just up the road from me," she said looking back at Nathan.

"What did he say?" asked Jonathan.

"He said that after Thursday night the thing you were talking about will not be a problem anymore. You'll enjoy being just sixth graders again, after he spends some time getting things ready," Terry said. "I'm not sure what that means but he told me you'd understand."

"Yes, something is going to happen and I'm afraid it won't turn out as Mr. Hawkins plans," Nicholas replied as he looked directly into Terry's eyes.

"Sorry to disagree with you, Terry. I know you understand exactly what is going to happen, at least you think you do," Jonathan added as Terry for the first time seemed uncomfortable.

"I'm not sure what this conversation is about but from what I'm hearing, it seems that both you and Mr. Hawkins may need to be very careful," their dad said.

"Well, I was just being friendly and passing along a message," Terry said as she turned and walked away.

"She's an interesting lady. I sure hope everything's going to be all right, whatever that means," Dad said as he opened the Odyssey doors and they all climbed in.

When they arrived at the ranch, the triplets thanked their dad for the ride and headed up to Mikaia's room.

"She's up to something! She says something's going to happen on Thursday night, but I know it will happen tomorrow night," Nicholas said.

"You're right. She wants us in the tunnel tomorrow night because Sam will have everything set up tonight to cave in the cavern and some of the tunnels. He hopes to trap or ...destroy us! I could read her mind. Even Cryptic is going to be there!" Jonathan said.

"What are we going to do? How can we stop it?" exclaimed Nicholas.

Mikaia looked down and held her forehead. "I think I can help. Sam just met with Terry and is now driving his truck up to the old school. He has boxes of low powered explosives. He has a map of all the mining tunnels in the area...I can't see anything else right now."

"Wow, that was amazing," Nicholas said.

"We can all thank the Master Inventor for that!" said Jonathan.

"Together we can see most of their moves. Hopefully, Mikaia can let us know what she sees when we go into the tunnels tomorrow night," said Nicholas.

"Do we really have to go?" Mikaia asked.

"If we're going to protect the old school and its powers, we do," Jonathan said.

"But Cryptic means to kill us!" Mikaia cried.

"I don't think that is going to happen," Nicholas replied. "Like I told Terry it's not going to turn out as Mr. Hawkins plans."

"What about Cryptic's plans?" Mikaia asked. "He knows that Terry and his Followers have not been able to do anything but annoy us these last few weeks, so he's bound to have some plans of his own! That's the part that scares me!"

"You're right. We'll need to figure it out to be safe. I'll keep trying to look into the future and you keep searching your visions, especially for Cryptic!" Nicholas suggested.

"They still don't know we can use the hand-slide sign and pop through time!" said Jonathan.

"That may be our greatest asset," Nicholas said.

"Or our greatest defense," Mikaia added.

"Don't you think we should pop over and see where Sam is placing the explosives?" asked Jonathan.

"That would certainly help," Nicholas replied. "I'll grab the flashlights and some wire cutters just in case we can destroy some of the charges, especially ones around the machine and old school."

"After what Terry told us today, he's not expecting us to check out the tunnel until tomorrow night," Jonathan explained.

"You're probably right," Nicholas replied. "Mikaia, are you coming?"

"Of course, we're supposed to stick together," she said as she picked up a flashlight.

"Okay, now think of the tunnel just before it reaches the Hole in the Mountain Mine junction. We'll sneak up the tunnel from there and see what he's doing," Nicholas said.

"Altogether now make the hand-slide sign and think of the tunnel and why we need to go there," Mikaia said and three pops sounded.

"Good, we're all here," Nicholas said as he turned on his flashlight and looked around. "There's where the Hole in the Mountain tunnel comes in. Let's move quietly up towards the invisible curtain."

The triplets moved slowly up the tunnel until they came to the curtain and turned off their flashlights. Nicholas peeked in for a moment then backed out.

"Sam's in there all right. It looked like he was placing charges around the sides of the cavern. I didn't see him attaching any wires to them. They may be radio-controlled explosives!"

"Has he placed any near the machine?" asked Jonathan.

"I couldn't tell, but he seems to have a box of them."

"You'd better watch him carefully," Mikaia said. "He's probably going to come out through the curtains and place some in this tunnel."

"Jonathan, you peek in and see what he's doing. If he starts to work his way towards the curtain, then move down the tunnel and see where he puts the others. I think I'll take a trip to his truck. He parked by the old school," Nicholas said and they heard a pop.

Nicholas appeared in the bushes behind the old school and cautiously worked his way over to Sam's truck. On the front seat he saw what he was looking for. He reached in and picked up the radio control unit that Sam was going to use to set off the explosives. It was set to channel five. Then he worked his way over to the old school and looked in the window. He didn't see any charges placed inside but figured if Sam was going to set some there he would do it on his way out. With that he made the hand-slide sign and popped back to the curtain just as Jonathan and Mikaia were starting back down the tunnel.

"He's on his way this direction," Jonathan said. They moved down the tunnel just as Sam appeared through the curtain.

He stopped at the opening and placed a charge above the curtain as he mumbled something about taking the whole thing down.

The triplets kept backing down the tunnel. Sam stopped now and then and attached a charge in a strategic location. He did this all the way back to the Hole in the Mountain tunnel. Then he also placed several charges at the junction to block the Creekside Mine tunnel. He started back saying something to himself about driving around to the opening of the Hole in the Mountain Mine and blowing that entrance too.

"Let's follow him back and cut the small antennas sticking out of each explosive we find," Nicholas said.

"That's what we're here for," replied Jonathan. "Besides I don't want the ceiling falling in on me tomorrow night!"

They slowly worked their way back up the tunnel trying not to miss any of the charges Sam had set.

"These things must have cost a fortune!" Jonathan said as he reached up and clipped off the antenna tip on another explosive charge.

"Be sure you clip enough off so it can't receive a

radio signal but not so much as to make it look like it's been tampered with, just in case Sam comes back to check them," Nicholas suggested.

When they came to the cavern, they carefully looked in. Jonathan went in first and worked his way over to the tunnel that led to the old school. Not seeing Sam, he climbed up the ladder to the cabinet and looked out. He could hear the sound of Sam's truck moving away from the school.

"He's gone," he reported as he walked back into the cavern. "Did he set charges on the machine?"

"I haven't found any inside the invisible shield or on it," said Nicholas closely examining the machine.

"Great! Then the Followers haven't discovered it," replied Jonathan.

"Yeah, but he has set a lot of them all through the cavern. Depending upon how powerful each charge is and its location, it could bring the whole ceiling down on it and not just shatter the quartz and walls," Mikaia said looking around.

"Then let's get the wire cutters working," Nicholas replied.

"I sure hope we can find all of them. I'm afraid we may have missed some in the dark tunnel, using just a flashlight," Mikaia said while carefully examining the cavern wall.

"I'd like to see the expression on Sam and Terry's faces when their charges don't go off tomorrow night with Cryptic looking on," said Jonathan.

"That's something I'm hoping not to see. The thought of even being in the same place with Cryptic and the pure evil he radiates scares me to death!" Mikaia said.

"I sure wish you wouldn't put it that way, Mikaia!" Nicholas replied.

After snipping off about twenty antennas in the cavern, the triplets worked their way up the ladder and into the old school.

"I don't think he left any in here," said Jonathan.

"Just the two he placed at the base of the ladder," Nicholas replied.

"I guess they're trying to make it look like some natural cave-in. I'm still concerned that we may have missed some," said Mikaia as she placed her hands on her forehead and looked down.

"Do you see something?" asked Jonathan.

"Yes, I see a man in a suit...I see others who I can't make out in the darkness...I see confusion and people running...and some loud noises...and..."

"Mikaia! Are you all right?" Nicholas asked as he grabbed her shoulders to hold her up.

"Yes, I'm just feeling a little dizzy and faint, but I'm fine."

"What do you think all that was?" Jonathan asked.

"I'm not sure. It could be tomorrow night, but I couldn't see any faces or make out a tunnel or cavern."

"Let's go back to your room right away so you can lie down," said Nicholas.

"Okay," Jonathan said. "Let's all make the hand-slide signal and think of Mikaia's room."

Three popping noises filled the empty school.

"Why don't we take it easy the rest of the afternoon and evening," Nicholas said. "We have a very busy day with the tour tomorrow and a very busy evening with…"

"Cryptic and his Followers!" Jonathan said as he finished Nicholas's sentence and Mikaia laid down on her bed.

"I agree," said Mikaia closing her eyes.

Chapter Seventeen

The Tour

The next morning none of the triplets were up at their usual times. Their mom had made blueberry muffins with a mixed fruit bowl for breakfast and needed to place the muffins in a warmer while she waited for them to come down to the kitchen.

Jonathan was the first down, following the freshly baked muffin smell right to the warmer.

"Good morning, Mom," he said. "Those muffins sure smell good."

"Have a seat and I'll pull some out of the warmer," she said as Nicholas appeared and sat down across from Jonathan.

"You both look tired," their mom said, "even though it's almost nine-thirty."

"I just couldn't fall asleep until really late last night," replied Jonathan.

"The same for me...just couldn't sleep," Nicholas added. He picked up a warm muffin and began to butter it.

"Nine-thirty?" Jonathan suddenly said.

"Yes, it's nine-thirty," she replied as Mikaia came

in with her arms above her head as she yawned and stretched.

"Mike and Ashlee are coming to pick us up in only half an hour!" Mikaia exclaimed as her yawn quickly turned into a look of pure terror. "I have to take a shower, dry my hair, and get out my clothes! I can't have muffins!" She turned around and ran back up the stairs.

"Girls!" Jonathan said picking up his second muffin and taking a bite.

Right at ten Mike Wilson pulled the Suburban up in front of the house. Ashlee, Marie and Larry were with him. The triplets walked out to the car as Larry pushed the door open.

"We really appreciate all of you taking your time to show us around," Mikaia said as she slid in the back next to Jonathan and Marie, "especially you, Mike, for driving."

"It's my pleasure. Without the three of you we might have been short one person today." He looked in his rear-view mirror and smiled as Ashlee smiled back.

"Where are you taking us first?" asked Nicholas, finding himself next to Ashlee in the middle row.

"We're going north on Highway 49 to show you a couple of warm weather hangouts," Ashlee said. Nicholas felt his side of the seat get a little narrower when Ashlee leaned towards him as the Suburban turned down the road.

"The first place is just outside of town on the North Fork of the Merced River that bends around Opportunity. There is a nice stretch of river where it slows down along a sandy beach," added Larry, who was sitting in the front seat next to Mike.

"This is great!" Jonathan said. "We know the town quite well, but we really haven't spent any time looking around the whole area."

"Well there's our home for the next three years," Larry said as they passed Lowe Middle School. "It has some fun teachers and all kinds of sports and activity programs for us."

A couple miles up the road Mike took a quick left and pulled up along the river.

"Here's the place I just told you about," said Larry as they all got out for a look. "You can see it's a safe swimming area with a beach. Those two tall trees along the bank over there have three rope swings that can take you almost to the middle of the river before you drop off into the water. That's my favorite spot when it gets really hot in the summer. You'll see a lot of kids from our school hanging out here."

As they all started to get back into the Suburban, Jonathan jumped into the middle of the back seat and made a ringing noise.

"What was that noise?" Marie asked as Jonathan turned red.

"Oh...it's just a little good luck charm I carry with me sometimes," he said. He pulled out the small brass bell with its short wooden handle to show her.

"I like that," Marie said as she took it and rang it once. "It makes me feel happy! I would have thought you'd have a rabbit's foot for a good luck charm."

"That's what I was looking for when I felt I needed good luck. When I finally spotted a rabbit behind our house, I found out how fast they can run and I finally gave up. The bell was easier to grab and much less painful to the rabbit," added Jonathan and everyone laughed.

They drove a few blocks down a winding road that ended at a large lake.

"This is Lake McClure, a fabulous place for water and jet skiing," Ashlee said. "You should come with my family sometime when we take our jet skis here for a ride. It's a lot of fun."

"You're really lucky to have places like these nearby. We didn't have them in San Francisco," Jonathan said.

"But you had ocean beaches and sailing, didn't you?" Larry asked.

"Yeah, but the bay water is freezing and we didn't do much sailing," Jonathan replied.

A few minutes later Mike drove south down Highway 49 heading through town.

"You already know about the Café and Grill and the Ice Cream and Candy Shop," said Ashlee. "When we're in town we go to either one of those two places."

"Unless, of course we go to the south side of

town," added Marie. "Then we hang out at Wong's Pizza."

Jonathan looked at Marie and smiled. He could tell that she was thinking how much she liked him. This made him smile even more, since he liked her too.

"Wong's really does make the best pizza in the world," Larry said.

"I don't know. In San Francisco, it would have been Giuseppe's Pizza. I keep thinking that Wong's Pizza could have too much soy sauce on it," Jonathan replied and everyone laughed.

"You'll find out soon enough! After our tour we're going there for lunch!" Mike said, "and it's on me!" he added and the group cheered.

"Thanks Mike. You've made Wong's Pizzas taste better already," said Jonathan as the rest of them laughed again, especially Marie.

About two miles south of town Mike turned in through an entrance gate that read "Mariposa County Regional Park" and stopped the Suburban. They all got out.

"If you're going to be playing soccer, Mikaia, you'll be spending a lot of time here. This is the home field for a lot of our school and community soccer teams," Ashlee said.

"And some great pickup basketball games, tennis, volleyball, and a big skate park!" Larry said as he pointed around.

"A lot of us have birthday parties and picnics here too over at those tables and barbecue pits under the trees," Marie said as she reached over and used Jonathan's hand to point. Jonathan eagerly let her. "My birthday's just a few days from now," she added.

"This is a beautiful park," Mikaia said. "It reminds me a little of Golden Gate Park in San Francisco, but it's not as big."

"Hop back in. There's one more stop before Wong's and his special soy sauce pizza with bamboo shoots and water chestnuts," Mike said.

Jonathan looked up in surprise and said," No, not really?" and everyone laughed again.

A couple more miles down the highway they came to a large shopping center.

"This is the place you come when you want some new clothes and things, Mikaia," said Ashlee. "It's about the only place you can get the latest fashions, at least the latest fashions for around here," she added. "It's our miniature version of a shopping mall, but you'll still find just about everything you might want here."

"I do recognize some of the major chain stores," Mikaia said as Mike drove them around the center.

"Does it have an electronics store?" asked Nicholas.

"Yes, a large one," Mike replied.

"Could you drop me there for a few minutes?" Nicholas asked.

"Good idea," said Ashlee, "There's this fabulous dress shop right next to it that I want to show Mikaia."

"And I want to show Jonathan something he'd really like," added Marie.

"What's that?" Jonathan asked.

"The Ultimate Ice Cream Store!" Marie said.

"Ultimate? I'd really like to see that!" Jonathan responded as Mike pulled up in front of the electronics store. He told them he'd wait for ten minutes and they jumped out of the Suburban.

Ashlee and Mikaia were the first to come back, followed by Marie and Jonathan. Apparently, Marie had to do some fast talking to stop Jonathan from ordering the specialty All-You-Can-Eat Hot Fudge Sundae. Using the argument that he wouldn't have enough time to finish it, even if she helped, and the fact that they would be stopping at Wong's Pizza in fifteen minutes for lunch, Jonathan was finally convinced ice cream wasn't a good idea. Shortly after Nicholas arrived, Mike drove out onto the highway.

"Did you get what you wanted?" Mike asked. Nicholas held up a bag and nodded.

"Are those the main hang outs you wanted to show us?" asked Jonathan.

"That's most of them, but we still have a couple of secret places we'll show you later," said Larry.

"Probably after I go back to college, right, Larry?" Mike asked as he turned out of the center and headed north.

"You've got it, Mike. A secret place is a secret place," replied Larry.

"Thanks guys for the vote of confidence," he said.

"After all you have crossed over, now being a college guy and all," Ashlee replied as she and Mike both smiled.

At Wong's Mike ordered two large pizzas with soy sauce, bamboo shoots and water chestnuts. The girl at the counter wasn't sure what to write down as the rest of them laughed. They finally agreed to a large pepperoni and a large sausage with extra cheese and sat down at a long wooden table. They had a lot of fun visiting and telling jokes. Jonathan had to admit that Wong's pizza was one of the best pizzas he'd ever had.

Nicholas suddenly became quiet as he felt a strange, yet sharp feeling surge through his body. It was like he'd accidentally put his finger in a wall socket. He managed to smile but he had this tremendous urge to run and hide, anywhere. He breathed in deeply a few times and realized it probably had something to do with tonight, something to do with...Cryptic.

Mike dropped the triplets off at two. After they thanked Ashlee, Marie, and Larry for showing them their hang outs. Ashlee reminded Nicholas about the dance party she was planning and Marie invited them to her birthday party at the park in a few days.

"That was a lot of fun!" said Jonathan, as they

walked up the stairs into their house. "Now we know some other places to go."

"It would have been a lot more fun if we didn't have a meeting with Cryptic tonight to save the old school and its power," Nicholas said.

"Yeah, I'd almost forgot," Jonathan said, his smile quickly turning into a frown.

"We need to think about how we're going to handle things tonight and plan what we should do if different situations develop," Mikaia said as they entered her bedroom.

"I say we get to the cavern early and check the explosives again. I want to make sure Sam hasn't planted more or found out we disabled the others," suggested Jonathan.

"Good idea!" replied Nicholas.

"We can check things out, then either pop or climb back up into the old school. That may be the safest place if Cryptic doesn't want it destroyed. Destroying the old school would let everyone know the cave-ins weren't accidental," Mikaia said.

"If Cryptic and his Followers see that we can block them from destroying the old school's powers, they may just leave us and the machine alone. We can always dazzle them by disappearing and reappearing around the cavern and old school," Mikaia said.

"Or all reappear back here if it gets to be something we can't handle," Nicholas added.

"Then it's all set!" Jonathan said. "So let's grab an

early dinner and be on our way."

"We just finished pizza a short time ago!" stated Mikaia. "Sometimes I feel you think with your stomach!"

"No, he's right," said Nicholas. "I sense we need to get there soon...that Terry and Sam are preparing to go to the old school now!"

"See! Let's grab a flashlight, the clippers, and a sandwich and then go. Being a custodian of the old school makes me hungry. Anyway, we could be there for a while," Jonathan said as he descended to the kitchen.

"Where are you three off to?" their father asked as they walked into the kitchen.

"We just thought we'd go over to the old school," Mikaia replied, "after we grab a sandwich."

"I see," he replied. "Should I tell your mother to have an early or late dinner?"

"Probably late," replied Mikaia.

"How was your tour with Mike and Ashlee?"

"We found some awesome places we didn't know about, where a lot of the kids hang out," Nicholas replied.

"And an ultimate ice cream store and a great pizza shop!" Jonathan added.

"I'm glad you had a good time," their dad said. "You three always seem to do well when you trust your instincts and stick together."

"You're right, Dad. We do!" Nicholas replied.

Chapter Eighteen

Cryptic

The triplets walked out towards the barn and once they were behind it, made the hand-slide sign and popped into the cavern.

"The cavern seems to be glowing more than usual," Mikaia said.

Quickly they walked over to the time travel machine and moved through its invisible shield.

"Just as I thought," Nicholas said. "It looks like Sam did come back and somehow found the machine! Look, there are several charges around its base. I'll just clip their antennas," Nicholas said. He slipped something next to the machine as Jonathan and Mikaia checked the other explosive charges in the cavern.

"He didn't discover that we had already clipped these," said Jonathan as he closely examined several with Nicholas at his side.

"I still hope we got all of them," Mikaia said. She heard a noise and turned.

"Got all of what, dear?" she heard Terry saying.

The triplets hadn't seen Terry and Sam come in from the old school tunnel.

"Oh," Mikaia said in surprise, "just some of the old quartz we'd picked up from around the cavern."

"So it had nothing to do with the old school's source of power, did it?" Terry asked as she and Sam came closer. "We'll just take a look to be sure that old machine under the invisible shield is all ready to really disappear."

"How did you discover it?" asked Nicholas.

"When I shared with you about Sam planning the tunnel's destruction on Thursday, apparently Cryptic was reading your minds through me, as we talked. I didn't know that then, until he told me you'd discovered the machine and where it was. He is so powerful and never ceases to amaze me," Terry said with a smile as both she and Sam started moving towards the machine.

At that moment the triplets, who were across the cave, all made the hand-slide sign and popped away and then a second later reappeared with a pop just in front of the machine blocking Sam and Terry's way.

"What? You can travel without the swing, slide, or merry-go-round?" Terry said surprised.

"I guess a lot of things never cease to amaze you!" replied Jonathan.

"You've gained more power than I expected, but you still won't be able to stop us from destroying the tunnels and machine," she yelled in her angry high-pitched voice.

"Sam!" Jonathan yelled, "don't even think of trying to charge through us to check the machine. We will stop you!"

"How'd you know...See, Terry, I told you they could read minds too," Sam said, stepping back.

"And mind reading," Terry said as she shook her head and frowned.

Nicholas looked down for a moment before he said, "And it looks like your evil friend is coming to help you since he feels you two can't seem to handle things yourselves." He looked into Terry's angry red eyes.

"You think your new powers are so great!" yelled Terry. "You'll soon see the full power of evil!"

All of a sudden there was a distinct smell of burning sulfur as a very pleasant male voice said, "Was someone talking about me?"

Walking up behind Sam and Terry was the typical storybook tall, dark and handsome man, wearing a designer dark suit and tie with a pearl white long-sleeved shirt accented by gold cuff links. The triplets just stood there for a moment in awe.

"Who are...what are...?" Jonathan tried to say.

"You didn't expect someone with horns, a tail, and a pitch fork, did you?" he said. "I only dress like that on Halloween! I gain a lot more Followers by using charm and pleasantries than threats and violence, although I do enjoy using the latter for my own amusement when I have to!"

"Then you're Cryptic?" asked Nicholas.

"That's a strange question coming from you, Nicholas, since you just foretold my presence! My, my, has the Master Inventor gotten carried away with the powers he's allowed you three to have!"

"He trusts us and we have faith in Him and in the power of His truth and love," said Mikaia.

"That's very nicely said, Mikaia. You've been taught well! You've also become quite a nuisance to me. You've even driven away some of my Followers, although Pete Rider and the Stewards will simply be replaced by other Followers that I have in the area," Cryptic said with a pleasant smile.

"You have other Followers in Opportunity?" Terry asked.

"You think that I'd not have others whom I could quickly bring in to take your or anyone else's place if that were necessary?" asked Cryptic.

"Well...yes I guess so, I didn't mean it that way" Terry sputtered back in reply.

"Besides, did you expect me to be pleased with your continued incompetence?" he asked.

"We did get the charges to blow up the tunnels and the machine set up for you," Sam answered, trying to show his loyalty and competence.

"Matter of fact, here's the radio controller that will signal the charges to blow," Sam continued as he handed Cryptic the controls.

"Well this may make amends for some of your imbecilic actions," he said as he held up the controls. "Even though I know you three don't need the power of the old school to travel, I think it's about time that all of this is 'accidentally' destroyed by a series of cave-ins. Since you have your own power to time travel, thanks to the continued interference of the Master Inventor, you should be destroyed with it. Then my Followers can continue their collection of weak and selfish people for my continued enjoyment."

"If it's okay with you, we'll let you take it from here," Sam exclaimed as he and Terry made a quick exit up the old school tunnel.

"It's so hard to get good help these days," Cryptic said just as the triplets started to put their hands together to make the hand-slide sign.

All at once they felt their arms held down at their sides. They turned and saw standing behind each of them a tall man wearing a red suit and tie with the same pearl white long-sleeved shirts with gold cuff links as Cryptic was wearing.

"You didn't think I'd let you pop away from all this fun did you? Besides, you're not foolish enough to believe that you're the only ones to read minds, are you?"

For the first time, fear appeared across the triplets' faces.

"By the way, I'd like you to meet three of my

Apprentices. They're kind of like you with the Master Inventor, you know, learning the trade," Cryptic said with a long laugh.

"With my protection, when the charges go off, we'll be fine! As for you, well let's just say you won't," Cryptic added as he held up the radio.

All of a sudden there were three almost deafening pops as Halo, Henry, and the triplets' father appeared behind each Apprentice, pulling their arms back to immediately release the triplets.

"Now sign!" Halo yelled and then there was a series of loud pops.

The triplets looked around and realized that they were in the old school. On the far side they could see a fearful Terry and Sam. Standing next to them were Halo, his son, Henry, and Nathan, their dad.

"Dad!" shouted Mikaia. "What are you doing here?"

"Just trust Halo and we'll talk later," he replied.

Cryptic and his three Apprentices appeared.

"Somehow I knew you'd show up. But I have to admit you did surprise me a little, Halo!" Cryptic said angrily, his smile gone.

"Yes, I know. The work of evil is never done," replied Halo. "You didn't really think the Master Inventor would let you destroy three of his future Guides, did you?"

"Oh! He has big plans for these three then. Pardon me but I still intend to stop all this foolishness," Cryptic said.

He held up the radio controls and pushed the send button.

Nothing happened, not a sound.

"So once again your Followers turn out to be the cream of the crop!" Halo said with a relieved laugh.

Cryptic tried pushing the button several more times before he threw the controls to the floor and gave Terry and Sam an icy look.

Then he looked back at the triplets and sneered. "So you, Nicholas, put a radio jamming device next to the machine...set to jam channel five I believe, how clever of you."

"I'll take care of that, sir," Terry said quickly. She crawled into the cabinet and headed down into the tunnel trying to redeem herself with Cryptic.

"You don't really think I need a radio device merely to set off an explosive charge, do you? I can simply direct a little flame of my own towards any charge I desire."

Cryptic sneered again and pointed toward the cabinet opening that Terry had just gone through. Everyone jumped when they heard an explosion. "Now you can't use that tunnel."

"But what about Terry?" a shocked Mikaia asked.

"As with most of my Followers, expendable if it means reaching my goals," Cryptic replied with a sickening smile.

Jonathan looked at Nicholas for a moment and

realized that Nicholas was so angry that he was going to charge Cryptic, so Jonathan instantly jumped forward too. Just as they reached out to grab him, two of his Apprentices jumped in front of Cryptic to protect him from the boys' attack. The bigger and stronger Apprentices locked their arms around them and held them in place.

"Well, well, bothered by that are you? Then let's blow another," he said as he pointed and a second explosion rattled from somewhere within the cavern.

With that, Halo held up both of his hands and commanded. "That's enough! Your games of destruction can no longer be tolerated!"

"Then I'll do another," Cryptic said as he pointed towards the cave. Nothing happened. In frustration he pointed again. Still nothing happened.

"What did you do?" he finally screamed at Halo.

"The Master Inventor gave me the power to neutralize you if I had to. Your evil powers are no longer usable here!" stated Halo severely.

"Then we'll use our physical strength and destroy the triplets!" Cryptic yelled.

The two Apprentices who were holding the boys began to tighten their grips around them so they couldn't breathe. The third Apprentice sprang towards Mikaia only to be stopped in midair by a powerful punch from Mikaia's father. Nathan held his foot across the prone and groggy man's throat so he couldn't move.

Cryptic was glowing with anger. The smell of sulfur was everywhere as he started towards Halo.

"Now would be a good time to ring that bell, Jonathan," Halo yelled.

Jonathan, who was getting dizzy, began to shake himself as hard as he could as the Apprentice fought to keep him in his grasp. Suddenly several rings emitted from Jonathan's front pocket. Immediately both Apprentices lost their grips and looked disoriented and faint.

"Ring it some more!" Halo shouted as Cryptic was almost upon him.

Jonathan quickly pulled the brass bell from his pocket and rang it as hard and fast as he could.

Instantly, Cryptic stopped in his tracks and grabbed at his throat as though trying to stop himself from being strangled. All three of his Apprentices were writhing on the ground in pain. Cryptic, in agony, slid to the ground with an expression of disbelief on his face.

"After eons of inflicting pain on others, is this the first time you've ever felt it yourself?" Halo asked.

Cryptic could only look back at him in silence.

"I call that my 'Golden Rule Bell,'" Halo added. "It was a gift to me from the Master Inventor. The bell simply gives to someone what they intend to give to others. If you'd wanted to give love, you would have received love upon its ringing. But since you intended extreme pain and even death, that's what you now will receive. Since the Master Inventor is also the force from which all grace comes, you will be spared. Yet, know this, I will entrust the bell to the three school custodians. It is another power that the Master Inventor desires them to possess."

Halo signaled for Jonathan to stop ringing the bell.

"Now you know what your evil feels like. We'll call it a well-deserved lesson for you. Now be gone before we ring it again!" Halo threatened as Cryptic and his three Apprentices, who were still bent over in pain, suddenly disappeared.

Everyone stood still for a moment. Sam Hawkins had run out of the old school and jumped into his truck as soon as Cryptic had fallen to the floor.

Nathan pulled the triplets together and put his arms around them telling them how proud he was of them.

"But what are you doing here with us?" Mikaia asked as a last few tears ran down her face.

"I've actually been with you all of the time," he said and he gave them another hug.

"Yes," Halo said. "He's the one who time traveled the other day to spy on Terry and her meeting in Sam Hawkins' storage room. That's how I knew what their plans were when we talked."

"You time traveled, Dad?" Jonathan asked in surprise.

"Yes, Son, I used the merry-go-round. That's all I

knew how to use."

"But how did you know...?" Nicholas started to ask.

"Your father was a student for two years in Opportunity almost thirty years ago. He also had a curious mind, adventure in his heart, and a caring soul and was selected to go on field trips. Your grandparents, his father and mother, commuted to work outside of town, so very few people in Opportunity got to know the Fraziers."

"But why did you move back here after all those years, Dad?" Mikaia asked.

"Several months ago, Halo contacted me, and told me that his son did not want to become the old school custodian. I knew how important that was to the community and the Master Inventor, much less to Harold Lowe. So we talked a long time about it and I knew that the three of you could grow into the job. All of you had the traits necessary to be successful. Your mother and I felt that the best gift we could give the three of you was to allow you to grow in the knowledge and love of the Master Inventor and gain the power to share this with others. So that's when Harold sold us his ranch and started the three of you on your journey. Your Mom and I always kept an eye on you."

"But what about Henry? He did come back," Nicholas asked as he took Henry's hand.

"It took me quite a while to learn what was

important in life, Nicholas," Henry said.

"Like I told you earlier, Henry just recently had second thoughts about what was important and now has decided to bring his family back to live in Opportunity. As you know, he time-traveled too. But both your Dad and Henry have none of the powers you have learned and been entrusted with. They can only go on a few field trips using the merry-go-round. When they both left many years ago, the playground became even more overgrown and wasn't used again until you three arrived.

Suddenly Mikaia spoke up, "But what happened to Terry? Did she get caught in the explosion?"

"You have the power to know, Mikaia, search your mind," Halo said.

Mikaia put her hand to her head and looked down. "Yes...I can see the cavern...Some of it has fallen in...the tunnel leading down from the old school...and the side of the cavern leading out through the invisible curtain to the tunnel that leads to our barn...but the time machine hasn't been disturbed!"

"What about Terry?" Nicholas asked. "Do you see her?"

"No, Nicholas, I don't," said Mikaia.

"Then she must have been caught under one of the cave-ins while she was trying to impress Cryptic and kill the three of you," Halo said.

"As I told you before, all life is important to the

Master Inventor and he mourns when any life is lost. Terry made choices and hurt many people over the years doing Cryptic's will. I can't say Opportunity will miss her...but they will probably never know who she really was. Many people in the community would have felt the tremors from the explosions and cave-ins. We'll pass the word around tomorrow that Terry was in the tunnels when the cave-ins occurred. People will assume she was looking for things for her antique shop and was probably killed when the mine collapsed. There is no purpose in telling them what she was really like and what she was really doing when it happened. Besides, the power of the old school and the good the three of you can do must be protected," Halo said.

"What about us, Halo?" asked Jonathan.

"You three are the custodians of the old school and will continue to take field trips and learn so you can help others and eventually become Guides for the Master Inventor."

"And what will we do about Cryptic?" asked Nicholas.

"Evil will always exist. We'll just continue to stop it whenever we can. As Cryptic said, there are and will be more Followers of his in and around Opportunity, especially as the community grows, but you'll be growing too. There are still some more things for you to learn and more things for you to find in the trunks. Although, I am surprised you missed your father and

Henry's initials on the newer clothes," Halo said with a smile as the triplets watched him disappear with a pop.

While the triplets walked back home with their dad, they were eager to talk.

"How did you get here tonight and how did you know where we were?" asked Jonathan.

"Halo had told me that he might need my help after I discovered the Followers' final plan and heard that Cryptic himself would come. That's when I found out that if Halo holds on to someone when he time travels, that person goes too! So he grabbed Henry and me and that's when we appeared!"

"I can't believe that you and Mom kept this quiet while we were going places and learning," said Mikaia.

"We knew that we must let Halo train and teach you. It was really hard to, as you say, 'play dumb', but we knew Halo would always keep you safe, as he'll continue to do."

When the triplets arrived home, they were greeted and hugged by their mom. Dinner was already on the table. They all had a long talk about everything that had happened to them since their arrival in Opportunity. As far as their parents were concerned, the triplets would continue to learn and grow in the ways of Halo and the Master Inventor, only now their parents could openly support them.

"This is still amazing to me. It seems so right, yet

so strange!" Mikaia said as she and her brothers sat on their front porch watching the sunset.

"To have all these powers and responsibilities seems like a lot to give a sixth grader," Jonathan replied.

"I'm afraid we won't be typical sixth graders," said Nicholas.

"Well, we can still have fun like sixth graders," Mikaia replied. "I know we will at Marie's birthday party in the park on Saturday."

"That does sound like fun," said Jonathan.

"She told me she was planning on having music so we could dance if we wanted," replied Mikaia with a big smile.

"Dance?" both boys asked at the same time.

Note from the Author

After writing *The Swing, the Slide, and the Merry-Go-Round,* my family and especially my grandchildren encouraged me to continue the story. I hadn't planned on doing so. However, I did feel that there was much more to the tale that could be told. So I wrote *The Triplets and the Power of The Old School,* and then I followed it with *The Triplets and Cryptic's Revenge.* These three books make up *An Old School House Mystery* series.

In books two and three, Nicholas, Jonathan, and Mikaia, as the new custodians of the old schoolhouse and its secrets, discover more evil Followers of Cryptic within their community and other unexpected places. As they gain knowledge and new powers, the triplets are able to solve the mystery of the old schoolhouse and save the school and their community from their evil nemesis, Cryptic.